# SURGEON STORIES

# PRAISE FOR DALY WALKER

With an insider's view of the medical profession, Daly Walker writes engaging stories, which often reveal their doctor-protagonists to be just as flawed and human as their patients. The result is an eye-opening collection of stories.

— BILLY COLLINS

This is among the best collections of stories I've encountered over the last decade or so—fiercely dramatic, immaculately composed, and so moving that even the most hardened heart must tremble. Treat yourself to the great beauty of *Surgeon Stories*.

— TIM O'BRIEN, AUTHOR OF *THE THINGS THEY CARRIED* AND *JULY, JULY*

Riveting and beautiful! With this collection of linked stories about the lives of surgeons, Daly walker joins the ranks of other great doctor-writers—Anton Chekhov, William Carlos Williams, Walker Percy, Ethan Canin—who understand the frailties of the human heart as well as they do the human body. His prose is as artful and precise as a surgeon's scalpel, and his skill is, more importantly, always in service of narratives that reveal not only his characters' fierce, frequently ambivalent, devotion to their medical vocations but also their rich, unsentimental, and deeply conflicted inner lives.

— K.L. COOK, AUTHOR OF *LAST CALL* AND
*LOVE SONGS FOR THE QUARANTINED*

Daly Walker has written a heartfelt book from deep experience. I admired its precision and quiet elegance.

— THOMAS MCGUANE, AUTHOR OF
*DRIVING ON THE RIM*

Crafted in language crisp and precise, *Surgeon Stories* delivers the kind of quiet tragedies that reaffirm the redemptive power of storytelling. Walker's unforgettable characters wrestle with hope and loss, love and regret, the exactness of science and the ambiguity of human emotion, and their struggles continue to haunt the reader long after their stories have ended.

— JOHN PIPKIN, AUTHOR OF *WOODSBURNER*

## ALSO BY DALY WALKER

# SURGEON STORIES

## FICTION BY

## DALY WALKER

Grand Canyon Press

TEMPE, ARIZONA

Grand Canyon Press
Tempe, AZ 85282
www.grandcanyonpress.com

Cover art, the painting "Theodor Billroth Operating," by Adalbert Seligmann. Cover design by Jonathan Weinert

Names: Walker, Daly, author.

Title: Surgeon stories : fiction / by Daly Walker.

Description: Revised edition. | Tempe, Arizona : Grand Canyon Press, [2021] | Revision of the 2010 edition published by Fleur-de-Lis Press.

Identifiers: ISBN: 978-1-951479-44-2 (hardback) | 978-1-951479-45-9 (paperback) | 978-1-951479-46-6 (epib) | 978-1-951479-47-3 (epub) | 978-1-951479-48-0 (iBook) | 978-1-951479-53-4 (Kindle) | 978-1-951479-58-9 (audio, individual) | 978-1-951479-59-6 (audio, library)

Subjects: LCSH: Physicians--Fiction. | Surgeons--Fiction. | Human body--Fiction. | Diseases--Fiction. | War--Fiction. | Compassion--Fiction. | Medical fiction, American. | Short stories, American. | LCGFT: Medical fiction. | Short stories.

Classification: LCC: PS3623.A35895 S87 2021 | DDC: 813/.6--dc23

Publisher's Note: This is a work of fiction. Names, characters, places, and incidents are a product of the author's imagination. Locales and public names are sometimes used for atmospheric purposes. Any

*Surgeon Stories* was first published by Fleur-de-Lis Press, 1436 James Court, Louisville, KY 40208 under ISBN number 978-0-9773861-6-1. The 2021 revised edition is published by Grand Canyon Press. The stories in this collection first appeared in the following magazines: "I Am the Grass" was published by *The Atlantic Monthly*; the stories "Sugar Cream Pie" and "If the Taste Is Bitter" were published in *The Louisville Review*; "Just Wine" appeared in *Mediphors*; "The Soothsayer" was first published in *The Hopewell Review*, and "The Donor" first appeared in *The Southampton Review*.

*To Toni Wolcott*

Surgery is the red flower that blooms among the leaves and thorns that are the rest of medicine.

— DR. RICHARD SELZER

What medicines do not heal, the lance will; what the lance does not heal, fire will.

— HIPPOCRATES

Surgeons must be very careful
    When they take the knife!
    Underneath their fine incisions
    Stirs the Culprit—Life!

— EMILY DICKINSON

There is no friend as loyal as a book.

— ERNEST HEMINGWAY

# CONTENTS

# I AM THE GRASS

BECAUSE I LOVE my wife and daughter and because I want them to believe I am a good man, I have never talked about my year as a grunt with the 25th Infantry in Vietnam. I cannot tell my thirteen-year-old that once, drunk on Ba Muoi Ba beer, I took a girl her age into a thatched roof hooch in Tay Ninh City and did her on a bamboo mat. I cannot tell my wife, who paints water-colors of songbirds, that on a search and destroy mission I emptied my M60 machine gun into two beautiful white egrets that were wading in the muddy water of a rice paddy. I cannot tell them how I sang "Happy Trails" as I shoved two wounded Viet Cong out the door of a medevac chopper hovering twenty feet above the tarmac of a battalion aid station. I cannot tell them how I lay in a ditch and with my M60 gunned down a farmer who I thought was a VC, nearly blowing his head off. I cannot tell them how I completed the decapitation with a machete, and then hung his head on a pole on top of a mountain called Nui Ba Dien. All of these things fester in me like the tiny fragment of shrapnel embedded in my skull, haunt me like the corpse of the slim young man I killed. I cannot talk about these things that I wish I could forget but know that I never will.

Twenty years have passed since the summer of 1968 when I flew home from the war and my "freedom bird" landed in the night at Travis Air Force base near San Francisco. I knew that in the city soldiers in uniform were taunted in the streets by flower children. So I slipped quietly into the restroom and changed from my dress khakis into jeans and a flannel shirt. Nobody was there to say, "Welcome home, soldier." It was as if I were an exile in my own country. I felt deceived and confused and, most of all angry, but I wasn't sure at whom to direct my anger or where to go or what to do, so I held everything inside and went about forming a life day by day.

After I was discharged from the army, I hung around Chicago for a couple of years among haunting memories and nameless faces. Devoid of hope or expectations, smoking dope and dreaming dreams of torment, I drifted from one meaningless endeavor to the next. I studied drawing at the Art Academy, cut grass on the grounds crew at Soldier Field, parked cars at the Four Seasons. Nothing seemed to matter, nothing changed what I was. I was still fire and smoke, a loaded gun, a dead survivor, a little girl on a bamboo rug, a headless corpse. I was still in the killing zone.

Gradually I grew weary of my hollowness, ran out of pity for my own self-pity. I wanted to take my life and shake it by the hair. I decided to use the GI Bill and give college a try.

I enrolled at the University of Wisconsin, the head-quarters of the Weatherman and the SDS, where I lived in a run-down rooming house on Mifflin Street among all the long-haired war protesters and scruffy peaceniks. During the day, I went to classes and worked as an orderly at a Catholic Hospital, but at night, after work, I went back to my room to study alone. Through the window, I could see mobs of students marching through the streets chanting, "Ho, Ho, Ho Chi Minh" and "Bring home the war." What did they know about war? I watched them, and I wanted to kick their hippie asses.

It was in caring for the patients at the hospital that I seemed to find what I had been searching for. While bathing or feeding a patient, I felt simply good. It was better than my best trips with Mary Jane. I decided to apply to medical school, and I was accepted.

One night when I was a senior med student, a couple of radical war protesters blew up the Army Mathematics

Research Center on campus. The explosion shook my bed in the hospital call-room like the rocket that blasted me out of sleep the night of the Tet Offensive. I have never been a brave man, and I lay there in the dark with my heart pounding, thinking I was back in Firebase Zulu the night we were overrun. A nurse called me to the emergency room to help resuscitate a theoretical physicist who had been pulled from under the rubble. His chest was crushed and both of his lungs were collapsed. He didn't need resuscitation. He needed a body bag. The war I was trying to escape had followed me home.

Now I practice plastic surgery in Lake Forest, a North Shore Chicago suburb of stone walls, German cars, and private clubs. On my arm is a scar from laser surgery that removed a tattoo I woke up with one morning in a Bangkok whorehouse. The tattoo was a cartoon in blue and red ink of a baby in diapers wearing an Army helmet and a parachute with the inscription "Airborne." I feel that I am two people at once, two people fighting within myself. One is a family man and physician who lives a comfortable external life. The other one is a war criminal with an atrophied soul. Nothing I do can revive it.

Even as a surgeon, I have a split personality. I sculpt women's bodies with breast augmentations, tummy tucks, face lifts, and liposuction. I like the money, but I'm bored with these patients and their vanity, their urgent need for surgical enhancement. I am also a reconstructive plastic surgeon who loves Z-plastying a scar from a dog bite on a little girl's cheek or skin grafting a burn on the neck of a small boy who fell against a space heater. I love reconstructing a lobster-claw deformity of the hand so a child can hold a spoon and fork. I'm no Albert Schweitzer, but every summer I spend a couple weeks in Haiti or Kenya, or Guatemala with Operation Smile, repairing cleft lips and palates. Removing the bandages and seeing the results of my skill sends a chill up my neck, makes me feel like something of a decent man, a healer.

TODAY, in late September, I sit in a window seat of a Thai Airway jet on its way from Bangkok to Ho Chi Minh City. I am headed to the Khan Hoa Hospital in Nha Trang for two weeks of my own little Operation Smile, repairing the cleft lips and palates of children on whose land I once wreaked havoc, whose parents and grandparents I murdered and who somewhere deep inside me, I still hold in contempt.

I stare out the airplane's window at tufts of white clouds that look like bursts of artillery flak, and I break into a sweat, remembering the descent of the airliner that flew me, a machine gunner, an Airborne Ranger, an eighteen-year-old, pissed-off, pot-smoking warrior, cannon-fodder, to Vietnam. The pilot lurched into a steep, spiraling dive to minimize the plane's exposure time to ground fire. I pitched forward in my seat, the belt cutting into my belly, my heart pounding. Until that moment, I had felt immortal, but then fear came to me in an image of my own death by a bullet to the brain, and I realized how little I mattered, how quickly and simply and anonymously the end could come. I believed that I would never return home to my room with the old oak dresser and corner desk that mother dusted and polished with lemon oil. Tears filled my eyes.

With the plane in a long gentle glide, I gaze out the window and search for remnants of the war. I see a green patchwork of rice paddies and fields of grass, the dirt roads whose iron red dust had choked me, whose mud had caked my jungle boots. A sampan floats down a river. Smoke curls lazily from a thatch roof shack. An ox pulls a cart. The land seems asleep and the war only a dream. I drop back in the seat, and I close my eyes. Stirring in my chest is the feeling that a dangerous, sleeping demon is awakening inside me.

I SPEND the night in Saigon at the Bong Song Hotel, a mildewing walkup not too far from the Museum of American War Crimes. The toilet doesn't flush. The ceiling fan croaks so loudly that I turn it off. Oily tropical heat drenches the room, and I can hear rats skittering across the floor. I feel like I once did trying to grab a little shuteye before going out on ambush patrol. I can't sleep. My mind is filled with the image of myself dragging the lifeless body of a kid named Dugan by the ankles through the mud.

In the orange light of dawn, I board an old minivan that will take me north to the hospital in Nha Trang. The tottering vehicle weaves through streets teeming with bicycles, cyclos, motor bikes, an occasional car. People gawk at me as if I were a zoo animal of a breed they have never seen before. The driver is Tran, a spindly man with wispy Ho Chi Minh chin whiskers. He has been assigned to be my guide and interpreter, but he is really the People's Committee watchdog. When I was here before, I would have called him a gook or a slope, a dink motherfucker, and those are the words that come to me now when I look at Tran. I picture his head on a pole.

We cross the Saigon River on Highway One, Vietnam's aorta, the artery connecting Hanoi with Saigon. The French called Highway One "la rue sans joie." We called it the "street to sorrow." During the war, I often traveled this road in convoys of trucks and tanks whose treads pulverized the pavement. I was always high on Buddha grass. Armed to the teeth. Frightened and mean. I was so young. I didn't know what I was doing here. A few miles out of Saigon, Tran slows and points to a vast empty plain overgrown with olive-drab grass and scrub brush.

"This Long Binh," he says.

"Stop," I say.

He pulls off the road and parks by a pile of rusty wire and scrap metal. I climb out of the van and stand, looking at acres of elephant grass blasted by the tropical sun. I think of Long Binh when it was an enormous military base, a sandbag city of tents, barbed wire and bunkers. We called it LBJ for Long Binh Jail. It was where I spent my first night "in country," sweat-soaked on a sagging cot, listening to the distant chunk of artillery, fear clawing at my chest. Now all I see is emptiness. There is nothing to verify my past, nothing to commune with. How hot it is. How quiet.

Since Nam, I have spent many nights with bottles of wine, reading the poetry of war—Homer and Kipling, Sandburg and Komunyakaa. Through the haze of my thoughts, words by Sandburg are moving. The words are about grass and war and soldiers in Austerlitz and Gettysburg and Waterloo, but they are about this place, too. "Shovel them under and let me work—I am the grass; I cover all." I gaze out at Long Binh's grass. It ripples in hot wind like folds of silk.

I climb back in the van, and we jostle on through rice paddies and rubber plantations, green groves of bamboo and banana trees. I have the strange feeling that my life has shrunk, that just around the bend an ambush will be waiting. I lean forward in my seat and ask Tran if he remembers Long Binh when the American soldiers were here.

"Vietnam believe it better not to remind of the past." He speaks, looking straight ahead through aviator sunglasses. "We live in present with eye on future." It sounds rote, like he is quoting from a propaganda paper. "Vietnam want to be thought of as country, not war, not just problem in other country's past."

On the berm, old women in conical hats spread rice and palm fronds to dry in the sun. Charcoal fumes waft from cooking fires. White-shirted children with red kerchiefs tied around their necks march to school. Two men, brown and bent as cashew nuts, face each other over a big teak log and pull a crosscut saw back and forth slowly, rhythmically. For a brief moment, the smell of gunpowder comes back to me, and I see little Asian men running headlong through tall grass, firing weapons and screaming. I see GIs running through smoke with green canvas stretchers.

THE ARRANGEMENTS for my mission in the coastal city of Nha Trang had been made through Dr. Lieh Viet

Dinh, the director of Khan Hoa Hospital. The morning after my arrival, Dinh sends word to my hotel that he wants to meet me for a welcoming dinner at a restaurant on the South China Sea. I have been told that Dinh was once in the North Vietnamese army and now is a high official in the province's Communist Party. What does he want? For me to say I'm sorry?

I hire a cyclo driver to pedal me to the restaurant. Mopeds with their exhaust tinting the air blue and bicycles piled high with cordwood tangle the streets. The Sunday afternoon sun is so bright it hurts my eyes. But there is a cool ocean breeze and the scent of bougainvillea in the air. Under flame trees with brilliant orange blossoms, barbers trim hair and clean wax from ears. Street vendors hawk flowers and loaves of French bread. Everywhere I look, I see Vietnamese getting on with their lives. I marvel at their serenity. They are no different from the people who I was taught to distrust, that I once machine-gunned. This street is no different from streets that I once helped fill with rubble and bodies. A man on a Honda raises his index finger and calls, "Hey, Joe. U.S. number one." I look away from him.

The restaurant is a rickety, tiled-roof pagoda perched on stilts over a beach of sand the color of crème brûlée. Below in a natural aquarium sand sharks and tropical fish dart among the rocks. In the distance, a soft vapor hangs over mountain islands in the bay. The restaurant is empty except for a gnarly little man sitting alone at a table with the sun splashing off turquoise water behind him. He is a militant figure with penetrating black eyes and hollow, acne-scarred cheeks that give him a look of toughness, a look that says, "You could never defeat me no matter how many bombs you drop." I know he is Dinh. The contempt that had boiled inside me during the war bubbles up. I can feel it in my chest.

He calls to me to join him. I settle into a wooden chair across from him and extend my hand for him to shake, but he ignores it and offers a stiff little bow of his head. Nervousness dries up the saliva in my mouth. A waitress in a blue ao dai brings us bottles of Ba Muoi Ba beer. With her lustrous black hair and slim silk-sheathed figure, she is beautiful and exotic like a tropical bird. The shy young girl with a dimple in her cheek that I took on the bamboo mat in Tay Ninh would be about her age now. I wonder what became of her.

In English that I have to listen to closely to understand, Dinh talks for a while about the Khan Hoa Hospital, the only hospital for the one million people of his province. He tells me that my visit has been advertised on television and that there will be thirty children with cleft lips to be repaired. His jaw tight, his voice intimidating, he tells me that the hospital has trouble getting medicine and equipment because of the American embargo. I pick up the bottle of beer and press it to my lips and tilt it. The liquid is warm with the slight formaldehyde taste that I remember from the war. I look at Dinh's slanty black eyes and stained teeth, thinking how easy it would be to kill him. I've been taught to do it with a gun or a knife or my hands. It would come back to me quickly, like sitting down at a piano and playing a song that you mastered a long time ago but haven't played in years. Suddenly, the thought of operating on little children in all this heat and dirt with archaic equipment jolts me back into the present. I ask him who will give the anesthesia.

"My doctors," he says. "Vietnamese doctors as good as any in the world."

The waitress brings bowls of rice and noodles and a platter of sea bass smothered in peppers, onions, and peanuts. She gives me chopsticks and Dinh a metal spoon. When we begin to eat, I see Dinh's hands for the first time. I am startled. Now I know why he didn't shake hands with me. His thumbs are missing. I watch him spoon rice onto his plate, clutching the utensil in his thumbless hand. He has learned a pinch grip between his second and third digits like children I have operated upon who were born with floating thumbs or congenital absence of the first metacarpal bone. Using his fingers as if they were tongs, he wraps the fish in a sheet of rice paper and dips it in nuoc cham sauce. The sauce smells rancid, and a sourness rises up my esophagus.

"I hear you in Vietnam during war," Dinh says between bites of fish and rice.

"Yes," I say. I can't take my eyes off of his hands.

"Where?" he asks.

"South of here along the Cambodian border near Tay Ninh."

"You see Nui Ba Den," he says. "How you call it? The black virgin mountain. This fish good. Dip your fish in nuoc cham."

I picture that black-haired man's head skewered on a bamboo pole.

"Yeah, I've seen Nui Ba Den," I say, feeling as if he must somehow know what I did on top of the mountain.

"Were you Army surgeon?"

"No. That was before I went to medical school. I was with the infantry." I take a gulp of beer. "That was a long time ago."

"Not so long ago," Dinh says. His lips curl into a smile that is filled with crooked yellow teeth. "Americans always think time longer than it is. Americans very impatient. Vietnamese very patient. We believe life is circle. Everything comes and goes. Why grasp and cling? Always things will come around again if you give them time. Patience is why we win victory."

In the filthy little village across the bay, I can see tin-roofed shacks, teeming streets, the haze of smoke from cooking fires—the thick stew of peasant life.

"How about you?" I ask. "Were you a doctor during the war?"

He wipes his mouth with his shirt sleeve and says, "In war against French colonialists, I was Vietminh infantry man. Fifteen years old."

He raises a maimed hand, and with a wave motion to demonstrate high altitude, tells how he twice climbed the mountains of Laos and Cambodia on the Ho Chi Minh Trail—once to fight the French and once to fight the Americans and their Vietnamese puppets. He was wounded at Dien Bien Phu. I wonder if that was when he lost his thumbs. I'm fascinated by his thumblessness. The ability to oppose a thumb and a finger is what sets us apart from lemurs and baboons.

"We have little to fight with," Dinh says. "After we shoot our guns, we pick up empty cartridges to use again. We eat nothing but tapioca roots and a half can of rice a day. For seven years, I fight hungry."

I listen to him tell of his wars, and it takes me back to mine. Cold-sweat nights peering out of a muddy bunker through concertina wire at tracers and shadows. Waiting. Listening. Grim patrols through elephant grass and jungle greased with moonlight. I can hear screams, see faces of the dead. What is memory and what is a dream? When it comes to the war, nothing seems true.

It seems impossible that something that tragic, that unspeakable, was once a part of my life. Suddenly I'm overwhelmed with emotion. I wonder if Dinh ever feels like crying. In the shallows below the restaurant, a sea turtle snaps at silver fish trapped in a net.

"How about in the war against America?" I ask. "Were you a doctor then?"

"I was surgeon in the war against you and your South Vietnamese puppets."

"Where did you serve? Were you in a hospital?"

"My hospital the forest. My operating table the soil of the jungle." He holds up both hands and rotates them for me to see. "I have thumbs then. I clever surgeon. I operate on everything from head to toes." He looks up at the ceiling as if there were an airplane circling overhead. "Your B-52s drop big bombs. They make earth shake. They scare hell out of me."

Dinh flashes a smile that makes me uncomfortable. He takes a drink of beer.

"Were you wounded?" I ask.

"You mean my hands?"

"Yeah. What happened?"

He rests them on the table, displaying them as he talks. He tells me that he was captured in the central highlands, not by Americans but by South Vietnamese Special Forces in their purple berets. When they learned he was a doctor, they chose him for torture. They tied him to a stake under merciless sun and every day pulled out one of his fingernails with a pair of pliers. At night they locked him up in a tiger cage. He speaks softly. On the eleventh day, they cut off his thumbs. Then they cooked them in a soup and told him to drink it. He hadn't eaten for two weeks, so he did.

"How did you survive?" I ask. "Why didn't you go crazy?"

"I pretended to be somewhere else. Somewhere at a time after our victory. I always knew we would win."

Dinh looks at my hands.

"You lucky," he says. "You have thumbs to do surgery. I can't even eat with chopsticks." He raises his hands, flexing his fingers. He glares at me with eyes that are hard and black as gun bores. "This should happen to no one."

We finish our meal in silence. Under the afternoon sun, the restaurant is stifling, and I feel queasy. I can only get down a little rice. But Dinh eats hungrily, shoveling in the food with the metal spoon as if to make up for all those years of rice and tapioca roots. When his plate is clean, he rinses his hands in a bowl of hot lime water with tea leaves floating on the surface.

He looks up at me and says, "To take the smell of fish from your skin."

∾

IN THE MORNING, I walk from my hotel through teeming streets and hot oily air to the hospital. Around the entryway, dozens of crippled peasants and ragged children with skin sores squat on the fine, powdered earth. Everything is dusty. I understand why Vietnam peasants call themselves "the dust of life." A boy with weightlifter arms calls to me in English from a bicycle that he pedals with his hands. He wants me to fix his paralyzed legs.

Khan Hoa's pale yellow facades give me the impression of cleanliness and light, but inside, the wards are dim and grungy, with no glass or screens in the windows to keep out flies and mosquitoes. Often two patients occupy a single narrow bed with family members sleeping nearby on the floor to assist with the feeding and bathing, the emptying of bed pans. A tiny, toothless woman with skin like teakwood waves a bamboo fan over a wasted man on a mattress without sheets. She gazes out at me with longing. Everywhere I go, someone with sorrowful eyes looks at me as if I were Jesus.

DURING MY FIRST WEEK, I don't have any more conversations with Dinh, but I see him every morning when he comes in his white lab coat to the surgery suite to watch me operate. At the door, he slips off his sandals and pads barefoot into the room, where he stands at the head of the table, his black eyes peering over the ether screen at the children whose lips are like hook-ripped fish mouths. He rarely speaks, and when he does, it is usually to address the Vietnamese doctors and nurses in a tone that suggests sarcasm.

It is impossible to know what his silence toward me means, but I become immersed in my work, and I don't worry about him. Once the operation starts, my concentration is complete, my only concern the child's face framed in blue towels and bathed in bright light. I have always been gifted at drawing and carving, and with a scalpel in my hand, I feel as if I am an artist, forming something beautiful out of chaos. I love mapping out flaps of skin around a child's mouth and then rotating them over the cleft to create a nice Cupid's bow of the lip with a clean vermilion border. My sutures are like the brush strokes of a portrait. Dinh must envy the collaboration between my brain and fingers.

Between cases I rest in the doctor's lounge at a wooden table. I drink a pot of pale tan tea, eat lichee fruit, and look out into the hospital courtyard that serves as the family waiting room. I often see Dinh with his hands hidden in the pockets of his lab coat, squatting in the dust, talking with the ragged parents of the cleft-lipped children who are undergoing surgery. His face, glistening under the hot sun, looks as if it has been linseed-oiled. His chronic scowl has become a comforting smile.

AT THE END of my first week, I call my wife and daughter to tell them that all is going well. When I report that I have repaired eighteen cleft lips without a complication, my wife seems proud of me. I am getting to like the nurses and doctors in the operating room. My feelings of guilt and ambivalence are being replaced by a sense of good will and atonement as if Vietnam and I were two bad people who have unexpectedly done something nice for each other. But on Sunday, Dinh sends word for me to meet him in his "cabinet," as he calls his private office. I worry that I have done something wrong.

The room is the size of an armoire and starkly furnished. A single bookcase contains the medical texts of the hospital's meager library. On the wall is a little green lizard and a yellowed photograph of Ho Chi Minh. From a cassette player on a homemade wooden table comes the music of a symphony orchestra playing Vivaldi's "The Four Seasons." The hospital sewer system has backed up, and the air smells brackish. My stomach churns. I sit in a straight-back chair across a metal desk from Dinh. My office in Lake Forest, with its oriental carpet and polished cherry furniture, seems infinitely far away.

"Vivaldi," I say to break the silence.

Dinh looks up from a journal article he is underlining with a wooden pencil. His face, shadowed by years of hardship, is expressionless. He wears a white shirt and a clip-on red rayon tie. He has a small Band-Aid on his chin where, I assume, he nicked himself shaving. I imagine him handling a razor, buttoning a shirt, tying a tie or shoestrings. Without a thumb's ability to pinch and oppose, even simple tasks must be difficult for him.

"Do you enjoy Vivaldi?" he asks.

"*The Four Seasons* is one of my favorites. When did you develop a taste for Western music?"

"When I was in medical school in Hanoi, French doctors play music in surgery room. Music only good thing about Frenchmen. Music good healing medicine. I play music to calm my patients."

He clicks off the tape and hands me the article he has been reading. It is a reprint from a French journal of hand surgery. I leaf through its pages, scanning illustrations that depict an operation in which a toe is transferred to the hand to replace a missing thumb.

"Can you make thumb?" Dinh asks.

I sit for a moment, remembering my last toe transplant, performed a couple of years ago. It was on a young farm boy who had lost his thumb in a corn picker.

"Yes," I say. "I've done this operation. Not often, but I've done it."

"I want you do this to me," Dinh says.

"Here? Now? You want me to make you a thumb?"

"Yes. I want you make me new thumb."

It is as if, fighting a losing battle, I suddenly see the enemy waving a white flag. For a moment, I look at his narrow, bony hand with the red ridges of scar where thumbs once protruded.

"It's a very hard operation," I say. " Quite delicate. A microvascular procedure. Even under perfect conditions it often doesn't work."

"I watch you operate." Dinh lowers his eyes and his voice. "You very careful surgeon. I know you can do."

"Let me see your hand."

He extends his right hand toward me. I rise and move around the desk. I take his hand in mine and turn it slowly, studying skin tone and temperature. His radial pulse bounds against my fingers. His nail beds are pink with good capillary circulation. The skin of the palm is creased and thickly callused.

"Thumb reconstruction must be carefully planned," I say. "You don't just jump into it. There are several techniques to consider."

In my mind, I review them: using a skin flap and a bone graft from the pelvis; pollicization in which the index finger is rotated to oppose the third finger; and my favorite technique which uses a tube graft of abdominal skin—but it has to be staged over several weeks.

"The new thumb must be free of pain," I say, carefully palpating the bones of his hand, searching for the missing thumb's metacarpal. I find it intact. "It has to have sensation so it can recognize objects. It has to be long enough to touch the tip of opposing digits. It must be flexible."

"You don't have to teach me," Dinh says, gruffly. "I know about this. I read everything in literature. Toe transplant best for me."

"I'm not so sure about that."

"Toe transplant best."

"Maybe so, but you're the patient this time. I'm the doctor. Let me decide."

I bend over and lift his dusty foot into my lap. I slip off his tire-tread sandal. His foot is the size of my daughter's, the toenails poorly cared for. My fingers find strong dorsalis pedis and posterior tibial pulses at the ankle. I would prefer to transplant the second toe but his is so small; I decide the big toe would make a better thumb.

"What you find?" he asks anxiously.

"You have good circulation and a metacarpal bone."

"So what you think? Toe transplant?"

I look up at Dinh's face. It is pale yellow, contrasting the density of shadowed books and wall behind him. His haughty eyes have softened into a look of hope and longing.

"I agree," I say. "A toe transplant would be best for you."

"You must do it then," he says.

"Maybe you could come to the States someday and have it done."

"I no rich American. No can get visa."

"There's a high chance the graft won't take. I don't have an operating microscope or some of the instruments I use."

He flexes and extends the four fingers on his right hand and smiles.

"Do it here tomorrow. I want to hold chopsticks again. I'm tired of eating like a Frenchman."

"Look," I say, "you don't realize how many things could go wrong."

"It work. I know it work."

I think how the fortunes of the Vietnamese always seem to be in the hands of others.

"Okay, I'll do it. A local anesthetic would be safest. Would that be all right?"

"Pain no matter. You do it."

"You're on. But don't be surprised if it doesn't work."

THAT NIGHT I lay awake under the mosquito net of my bed, reviewing the technique of toe transplantation, anastomosing in my mind, tendons and tiny digital nerves, minute veins and arteries. Tropical heat drenches me. The bark of dogs comes in from the street. When I finally fall asleep, I dream again of the man whose head I severed and stuck on the end of a pole. We meet in the Cao Dia Temple in Tay Ninh, a vast gaudy cathedral with a high vaulted ceiling, pillars wound with gilded dragons and pink serpents, and a giant eye over the altar. He stands naked in front of me, holding his head with its sheen of black hair in the crook of his elbow.

THE SURGERY SUITE IS HIGH-CEILINGED, with dirty windows and yellow tile walls, like the restroom of an old train station. The air is drowsy with the odor of ether that leaks from U.S. Army surplus anesthesia machines. Outside the operating room, I attach magnifying loupes to a pair of glasses. I focus the lenses on the lines of my fingertips and begin scrubbing my hands in cold water at an old porcelain sink. Through the door, I see Dinh under the thickness of drugs and strapped to the operating table. Bathed in fierce white lights, with his arms extended on boards at right angles to his body, he looks as if he has been crucified. I have sent an orderly to his office for his cassette recorder, and the melody of *The Four Seasons* plays softly at the head of the table.

For a moment, I rinse my hands, designing in my mind skin incisions and tendon transfers. In the past, to decrease operative time and diminish my fatigue, I used a second surgical team to prepare the recipient site in the hand while I dissected the donor tissue from the foot, but here I am alone.

With water dripping from my elbows, I step into the room. Suddenly I feel a surge of force, a sense of power that has been mine in no other place but surgery, except when my finger was on the trigger of an M60.

The instruments I have brought with me are arranged on trays and tables. My weapons are tenotomy scissors and mosquito hemostats, atraumatic forceps and spring-loaded needle holders. A scrub technician, who once worked as interpreter in a MASH unit during the war, hands me a towel. Two masked nurses prep Dinh's foot and hand with a soap solution. The surgery team's spirits are high. Listening to them talk is like hearing finches chirp.

Gowned and gloved, I sit on a stool beside Dinh's right hand. I adjust the light and begin the numbing with an injection of Xylocaine. The prick of the needle arouses him from his narcotized slumber, and he groans.

"Everyone ready? Let's go. Knife."

The nurse pops the handle of the scalpel into my palm. A stillness settles over me and passes into my hand.

Dissecting out the filamentous vessels and nerves that once brought blood and sensation to Dinh's missing thumb is tedious and takes over an hour. While I work, a nurse sits at Dinh's head, murmuring to him and wiping his forehead with a wet cloth. I wonder what Dinh is thinking. Is he remembering the men who cut off his thumb? Is he dreaming of what he might do if he met them again? When all the digital nerves and vessels and tendons are isolated and tagged with black silk sutures, I cover the hand with a sterile towel. Before I move to Dinh's foot to harvest his spare part, I step to the head of the table.

"It's going well," I say. "You all right?"

"Don't worry about Dinh," he says. "Worry about operation."

I make a circular incision around the base of the phalanx, taking care to preserve skin in the web space so the defect can be closed without a skin graft. When the toe is finally transected, with its trailing tentacles of tendons, nerves and vessels, it looks like a baby squid. I wrap it in a saline-soaked gauze and carry it to the hand. I'm tired and sweating. My back hurts. My eyes ache. I feel as if I were on a long, forced march.

First I join the bones, using wires to fuse the toe's

bone to the hand's metacarpal in a position of flexion and pronation, to provide Dinh with a good pinch. Next I unite the tendons with strong nylon sutures—extensor halicus longus to extensor pollicis longus, flexor hallucis longus to flexor pollicis longus.

Fighting off fatigue, I begin the most tedious and critical part of the procedure—the anastomosis of filamentous nerves and vessels. It is like sewing strands of hair together. Under the magnification of the lenses, the delicate instruments seem big and blunt, the slightest tremor of my fingers appears to be an awkward jerk. Blood oozes into the wound and obscures my vision. A few drops seem like a crimson flood.

"Suck. Will someone please suck."

I take a stitch in the digital artery, and Dinh's hand rises from the drapes. I push it down, pinning it to the table.

"Goddamn it," I say. "Hold still, Dinh."

"Dau," Dinh moans in pain. "Dau. Dau."

"He feel it," the nurse says.

"More Xylocaine," I say. His hand jerks again. "Hurry up, Goddamn it. Xylocaine."

After four hours, Dinh has a new thumb pinned in place by Kirschner wires through the bones and a neat ring of black nylon skin sutures. Exhausted, I sit for a moment cradling his hand in mine and staring at my work. The graft is cool and cadaveric, as pale as plaster, but it twitches slightly with his pulse. I haven't prayed in years, and doubt that it does any good, but I silently ask the Lord to give the transplant life. The nurse hands me a sterile dressing, and I wrap up his fingers in loose layers of fluffy gauze followed by a light cast of plaster of paris. I strip off my gloves and step to the head of the table. I look down at Dinh's face, resting my hand on his shoulder. His pitted cheeks puff with each breath, and his half-closed eyelids flutter.

"All done, Dinh," I say.

"How does it look?" he asks groggily.

"Like a thumb."

DINH BELIEVES our lives move in circles, repeating themselves endlessly like the four seasons, like the cycle of his country's rice crop. Planting. Weeding and waiting. Harvesting. Fallowness. Planting again. If things don't work out, so what? Another chance will come around, the way winter always gives in to spring. But I believe that my life is somehow outside these circles, that I am on a straight march toward something final, and on that journey to the end of existence, the journey itself is all there is. When I fail along the way, when something I need eludes me because of a mistake I have made, the mistake itself becomes a defeat, and I am left with only loss, with emptiness, uncertainty, and regret.

Because that is my nature, the fate of Dinh's transplanted toe takes on a monumental importance. I lie awake at night in unbearable heat, sweating and worrying about infection and thrombosis. Each morning, before I start my surgery schedule, I visit Dinh, in his stark hospital room with its metal cot and the clay pot that serves as a bedside commode. Peering up at me from his pillow through circular, Uncle Ho wire rims, he appears calm and confident, talking of all the things that will be easier for him to do with his new thumb— holding a pen when he writes haiku, picking hibiscus blooms for his wife's table, playing his bamboo flute, and of course, eating with chopsticks. He says he may even do a little minor surgery. The thought of him trying to operate makes me cringe.

One day I show him a few snapshots of my daughter. He leafs though the pictures and nods politely. Then he talks about all the children that I operated on who now can smile and suck their bottles. The children, tender and pliant, are what are important, he tells me, not old people like him, who have become dry and rigid and whose lives are behind them.

When I examine him, I am relieved to find that he is free of fever. His pain is minimal. The dressing smells clean and there is a little blood stain on the gauze, which is a good sign. The graft has to be taking. I begin to look forward to removing the dressing and seeing a nice new pink thumb. It will be a kind of miracle.

THE DAY before I am to leave Vietnam is the day of atonement, the time of truth, the moment to unwrap Dinh's hand and see if his thumb is viable. It is also the end of the rice harvest and the farmers are burning off the fields to the west of the city. As I walk to the hospital, I can see a gray haze of smoke hanging over a horizon curtained with flames. It is a scorched-earth image, reminiscent of napalm and war.

In the surgery clinic, I meet Dinh, sitting in a wheelchair with his bandaged hand in a sling and a confident smile on his face. Hoa, a petite nurse with a pretty smile and pearl earrings, places his hand on a white towel. A hush hangs over the room. My heart gallops. I cut the cast with heavy scissors and begin carefully unwinding the dressing. The gauze is stuck with dried blood, so I moisten it with saline and let it soak for a few minutes while I redress his foot. I am pleased to find the donor-site incision clean and healing well, but when I peel off the last layer of gauze from his hand, I smell the faint dead odor of necrosis. Dinh's new thumb is the cold clay color of mildewed meat. I feel his eyes on me. I want to leave now, get on an airplane and fly home, let someone else amputate the dead thumb, let someone else clean up my mess. I glance up at his face. He is staring at the dead toe. Goddamn this dirty little Job of a country. Nothing turns out right here. I look out the window. The monsoon season is only a few days away, and already it is raining. Big drops kick up dust like rifle fire.

"It doesn't look good," I say. "Maybe I should redress it and give it a little more time."

"Gangrene," he says. "It dead. Take it off."

IN THE OPERATING ROOM, everyone works in silence. On the table, Dinh looks small and fragile, exhausted as if he had just climbed one of those mountains on the Ho Chi Minh trail. I pull out the Kirschner wires from his hand with a hemostat and snip the nylon sutures. It is a bloodless operation. The dark necrotic transplant falls off onto blue drapes, stiff and cold, no longer a thumb or a toe. I can scarcely believe my childish hope that it would survive. I pick it up with sterile forceps and drop it into a stainless steel pan. I think of Dinh's torturers in their purple berets chopping off his thumbs with a big knife. I see him drinking soup made with his own flesh and bone.

THE DAY OF MY DEPARTURE, Dinh sends a driver in an old Toyota to take me to the airport. I am disappointed that he isn't riding with me, but something tells me he will be waiting for me in the terminal. I want to apologize to him because the toe transplant didn't work, and then have him laugh and say, no problem, that in his next life he will have thumbs.

I check my bags at the ticket counter and hurry to the lounge, hoping that Dinh will be waiting there in a rattan chair with his bandaged foot propped up while he drinks a cup of green tea. Over the door to the sunny room, a sign announces, NHA TRANG A GOOD PLACE FOR RESORT. With my heart hammering high in my chest, I step inside. No Dinh. The lounge is empty and silent except for the groan of a ceiling fan that churns warm, viscous air.

I move heavily between tables and out glass doors onto the tarmac. Silence surrounds me. The sun. The quiet blue sky. I stand for a while, gazing at tall brown grass and prickly pears that sprout through cracks in the airstrip. Concrete revetments built during the war to shelter American airplanes from rocket attacks are empty and crumbling, like mausoleums of an earlier civilization. Beside the runway rests the rusty carcass of a U.S. C-141 Starlifter. I watch an old U.S. F-4, now a

Vietnamese fighter jet with rocket launchers riveted to its wings, practice a touchdown. The plane bounces on the concrete, its tires screeching like the cry of some fierce predator. The gray gunship rises into sparkling blue sky. My eyes follow its flight until it disappears into the glare of the sun.

Soon an Air Vietnam passenger plane lands on the runway and taxies to the tarmac, where it shimmies to a stop. It is an old Russian turboprop with a dented fuselage and chipped blue and white paint. I have heard that Air Vietnam's planes were in poor repair because the airline has trouble getting parts and that Japanese businessmen refused to fly on the airline because of the danger.

I mount the steps into the aircraft. Inside the fuselage, heat and the oily odor of fuel squeeze the breath out of me. Only two other travelers are on board, a mamasan in a conical hat and her baby that she carries in a broad sling around her waist. She stands in the aisle swaying back and forth to rock the infant. I choose a window seat with tattered upholstery. Soon the engines on the wings cough and sputter to life. I try to buckle my seat belt, but the clasp doesn't work. I shake my head and smile. In Vietnam danger has always been ubiquitous, life tenuous. For some reason I welcome the risky ride. It makes me feel a part of the land.

# SUGAR CREAM PIE

INSIDE RUBY'S PIE SHOP, it is light and cool, the linoleum floor clean but worn. At a window table sits a balding surgeon with a mustache that he tints with Grecian Formula. His hands are pretty with long graceful fingers and manicured nails. He worries that his knuckles are beginning to show the first nodules of osteoarthritis. He left this little Indiana town thirty years ago, and he has returned to settle his mother's estate and retrieve a couple of her antiques, a wicker settee and a Windsor chair, for the waterfront townhouse where he lives with Raymond. While he toys with a red plastic tulip in a vase, he thinks how stagnant and Midwestern the town is, how provincial. It seems to have shrunk to something even smaller and less significant than he remembers. They never understood him here. Now that his mother is gone, he doubts he will ever return.

He stares at a man at the counter hunched over a cup of coffee. The man's long, greasy hair hides his face, and crutches are propped against the stool beside him. He reminds the surgeon of a derelict with a ruptured aorta that he recently operated on. The patient had a tattoo on his arm that said, "Born to Lose." These people, who seem to expect nothing from life and give little to it, create in the surgeon a clash of compassion with loathing.

Outside, the sky darkens, and the wind freshens. A waitress in a pink uniform with a little white apron comes to his table.

"It's going to be a goose drownder," she says. "Ready for dessert?"

"You bet." He winks at her. "Ruby still make that Hoosier sugar cream pie?"

"Sure does."

"That's what I'll have. Sugar cream pie."

She clears his plate and wipes away crumbs with a damp cloth.

"Keep your fork," she says.

The man at the counter lights a cigarette and coughs, then turns to watch rain drum against the window glass. The man's puffy face is white as paper and covered with a stubble of gray whiskers. For a moment, his eyes touch the surgeon's eyes. Then the man lowers his gaze as if he has seen something forbidden.

"No way," the surgeon says to himself. "It can't be him."

The waitress slides a piece of sugar cream pie in front of the surgeon. The desert is glazed with a caramelized layer of creamed butter, maple sugar, and a sprinkling of nutmeg. Its vanilla scent causes the surgeon's salivary glands to spasm.

"That Charlie Hutchins?" he asks in a low voice and nods toward the counter.

"Yeah." The waitress shakes her head with disgust. "That's Charlie, all right."

"Lord, I hardly recognized him. What happened to him?"

"Booze, sugar diabetes, hard luck, meanness. Who knows?"

With his knife, the surgeon cuts off the point from the wedge of pie. Deftly, he dissects the creamy filling from the crust the way he teases an atheromatous plaque from the wall of an obstructed carotid artery. He lifts the morsel to his mouth.

"Mmm," he says, tasting the rich sweetness. "A bite of heaven." With his fork, he gestures at the waitress passing by. "What'll you take for this recipe?"

"Sorry." The waitress smiles. "It ain't for sale."

The surgeon finishes his last bite of pie, then wipes

his mouth with a napkin. He makes his way to the counter and slips onto a stool next to the man.

"It's been awhile," the surgeon says.

"I thought that was you," Charlie answers without looking at the surgeon. "Where you at now?"

"San Francisco," the surgeon says.

He notices Charlie's dry skin and lips, his shallow rapid breathing. They tell him that Charlie has missed his morning insulin.

"Your mother," the surgeon asks, "how is she?"

"She's been gone for ten years."

"I'm sorry." The surgeon pauses for a moment, then says, "When I walked over the Salt Creek bridge yesterday, I thought of that tree house we built down there. Remember how we'd hide in it and smoke those grape vines?"

Charlie sips his coffee instead of answering.

"Why the crutches?" the surgeon asks.

Charlie spins on his stool. He lifts the leg of his pants and bares the bulbous, scarred stump of a below-the-knee amputation. The sight of the footless leg startles the surgeon. For an instant, a wave of sympathy washes over him.

Charlie flashes a smile that vanishes as quickly as it came.

"You do that to people?" he asks. "You a damn sawbones?"

The surgeon stiffens when he hears Charlie's voice. It echoes the same contempt it did on the long ago night when Charlie slammed him into a tree, slapped his face, kicked him in the balls, taunted him, "Fuck you, Queenie. You rich little queer. You fucking faggot. I know all about you."

"No," the surgeon says. "I'm a vascular surgeon. I clean out arteries. Repair aneurysms. Things like that."

He motions to the waitress.

"Bring me another piece of sugar cream. What about you, Charlie? Want something?'

"She'll get my coffee," Charlie says.

The waitress fills his cup. Charlie picks up a canister of sugar, then puts it down. He empties a packet of Sweet 'n Low into the coffee and stirs it with a spoon.

The surgeon looks through the window into a gray drizzle.

"The rain is letting up," he says. "I've got business to tend to. Think I'll make a dash for it." He rests his hand on Charlie's shoulder. "We're getting old," he says.

"Who gives a shit, man," Charlie says, pulling away from his touch.

Damn you, Charlie, the surgeon thinks, you're still a bastard.

"You want a doggy bag?' the waitress asks as he pays the bill. She points at the uneaten pie. "I'll wrap it up for you."

The surgeon watches Charlie glance at the wedge of pie with longing the way an alcoholic looks at a tumbler of whiskey. He smells Charlie's breath, sweet, like over-ripe fruit. He recognizes the odor of ketosis, the scent of diabetes out of control.

"No thanks," the surgeon says. "No doggy bag."

He nudges the sugar cream pie and a clean fork toward Charlie's coffee cup.

"Listen, Charlie, you take care of yourself. You hear?"

# THE NATURE OF LIGHT

CHASE IS AN OPHTHALMOLOGIST, the only female eye surgeon in southern Indiana. Her practice is one of the busiest in the state. In her clinic, she employees twenty-five people including an optometrist, two registered nurses, a certified public accountant, and an office manager with an MBA. She believes there are two essentials to happiness—work and love. Since the death of Rex, her only child, Chase is left with work alone. She is sustained by a single vision: to create a center of excellence in eye care.

When the work finally wears her down, she occasionally surrenders and takes Wednesdays off to rejuvenate herself. If the weather is foul, she spends this leisure time painting abstractions of the human eye. She uses acrylics of bright colors to create images of optic pathology: retinal detachments, floaters in the vitreous, the fluffy arterial patterns of diabetics. On sunny days she prefers to be outside working in her flower beds.

Today, Chase, in cutoff jeans and jogging shoes, carries a cup of coffee to the patio. Pale September sunlight floods her face and arms but doesn't warm them. Her head aches and her stomach is queasy from last night's tequila. She has taken Maalox, two aspirins, and a Compazine. From a distance, she hears a rumble like the sound of thunder, but the sky is rinsed-blue and cloudless. She realizes the noise echoes from practice airstrikes at the National Guard airbase several miles away. Chase is a member of Physicians for World Peace, and the idea of bombs exploding so near, interrupting the serenity of her home, disturbs her. She reminds herself to write her congressman about the bombing.

She goes into the garage and gathers up gardening supplies: a cultivator, insecticide, fertilizer, pruning shears. While she puts them in a garden cart, she pictures last night's argument with Ned—the drinking, then the name calling, the same old accusations, and finally Chase screaming that if it wasn't for Ned, Rex would never have been riding his bicycle that afternoon. She sees the blue ceramic pitcher, the one they bought on their honeymoon in Mexico, crashing to the floor; syrupy, green Margaritas puddling on terra cotta tile; Ned driving off, his tires spewing gravel.

Chase kneels on a slab of the patio's Pennsylvania blue slate. The stones are rough and cold against her knees. With the cultivator she claws the earth around a rose named Chicago Peace. In her mind's eye she sees the shards of blue pottery on the kitchen's floor. She feels shattered herself and ashamed.

She salts the loose earth with fertilizer and works the granules in, picturing herself last Saturday morning. In a starched white lab coat she stood in the front of the medical students in University Hospital's auditorium. She was presenting a grand round's lecture titled "Laser Theory and Application in Ophthalmology." She explained to the students how the energy of light in the form of a laser beam is focused onto abnormal vessels in a patient's retina to obliterate diseased arteries, preventing retinal detachment and eventually blindness. To illustrate points about transverse electromagnetic mode and monochromatic coherent light, she had flashed, onto a screen, pictures of Darth Vader and Han Solo dueling with laser swords.

As she prunes a rose with shriveled brown petals, she recalls feeling pleased with the way the talk had gone until a medical student, with ringlets of black hair and an earring, raised his hand and asked, "So what is the nature of this light?"

She was puzzled by the question. She thought he was acting smart, somehow trying to put her down because she was a woman. But it worried her that there was a question about light, the very nature of it, that she didn't have an answer for.

"I'm afraid that's not within the scope of this class," she said. "That will be it for today."

The student came down the stairs toward the podium, and she hurried out of the auditorium to avoid him.

As she works with her roses, it seems as if recently she is losing power and admiration, falling short in everything. She is no longer surprised by her failures.

Ned, in gym shorts and a gray T-shirt, ambles up the hill from his vegetable garden. Handsome, taut and athletic, he is a manufacturer's rep who makes a moderate income selling small parts to companies that make mufflers for automobiles. Sun angling through a tree makes shadowy patterns on his face.

For years Ned has been planting vegetables like bell peppers, sweet corn, and snap peas. But the soil he cultivates across the road from their house is stubborn southern-Indiana red clay with poor drainage and few nutrients. Tomatoes are the only decent vegetables from his garden that Chase remembers eating. She marvels at the satisfaction he seems to derive from common tomatoes. She tries to think of something to say to him to set things right, to put last night behind them, but she can't make herself begin.

"Your roses are kinda puny," he says, pointing at a leggy yellow hybrid tea.

Chase is relieved to hear him speak in a friendly tone.

"They're light-starved," she says. "This time of year the sun's more distant, its angle with the earth more acute. The light waves have less energy."

She squints toward the sky. The sun is pale, without power, without heat. She believes the angle of light controls everything. The seasons. Her biorhythms. Reality.

"I dread the end of summer," she says.

Chase sits in the grass and ties the lace on her New Balance jogging shoe. She likes to think in metaphors and find symbolism in everyday things. That's why she recently bought two pairs of New Balance running shoes, a pair for herself and a pair for Ned. She had said, "Here, Honey, New Balances to help us establish equilibrium and get our feet back under us. We need to do things together, get to know one another again. We should jog together."

IT WAS the summer before last, two weeks before Rex's twelfth birthday, when the lightning struck. The day was a sunny, benign Saturday. Rex had asked if he could go to a movie. Chase had said fine, no problem, as long as the movie wasn't rated R. But Ned had argued. He said the boy had no business being cooped up in the dark movie theater on such a nice day. Ned wanted Rex outside playing in the sunshine and fresh air. Rex didn't go to the movie. He rode his ten-speed down Tulip Lane under a flock of clouds, all fluffy and white except for one that was low and dark. This black mutation opened up with a shower that drenched Rex. He was splashing through a puddle when lighting struck. It burned his hands where they gripped the handle bars, his feet and bottom where they touched the pedals and the seat. It left him sprawled on the black asphalt with his heart stopped.

After the funeral Ned went backpacking alone in the mountains of Montana, eating lecithin wafers and trying meditation. While Ned was camping, Chase was in Honduras participating in Operation Sight. She donated her time at a clinic in the jungle, testing eyes, treating glaucoma and conjunctivitis, fitting glasses, performing cataract surgery. She was miserable. She saw Rex's dark brown eyes in the eyes of every child she examined.

After Ned and Chase came home they never jogged together or went to movies or out to eat at the country club. It was as if the lighting's electricity had polarized them with negative charges that repelled each other. Before she began painting, Chase tried jazzercise, then she switched to tap dancing. She danced to old songs like "Tea for Two" and "I Get a Kick Out of You." Ned started rowing, a one-man scull on the river in warm weather, a rowing machine in the basement when the water was frozen.

"YOU KNOW we ought to try running together," Chase says now. "The counselor wants us to spend time with each other."

"Jogging's hard on my knees. I'll stick to rowing," Ned says, looking off in the distance toward the rumble of the air strikes. "Remember we see the counselor today."

"Fun and games," Chase says, remembering last week's session. "I wonder what charade we'll play today?"

The marriage counselor, to get them talking, had asked what characters in literature they thought they were like. Chase had said *Jane Eyre* because Jane was artistic, melancholy, lived in Thornfield, and was controlled by Mr. Rochester. Ned had chuckled at the idea that she considered him the controller. He had compared himself to Viri in Salter's *Light Years*. A child had been killed. The dissolution of a marriage.

Ned leans down. From a rose he pinches a yellow leaf dotted with black spots.

"Fungus," Chase says, frowning. *"The War of Roses.* Another battle that I'm losing."

Ned discards the leaf. He does a couple of deep knee bends. Then he bends over to touch his toes, stretching his hamstrings and calf muscles. Chase notices his sculptured thighs and round firm buttocks beneath nylon shorts. She used to tell him that his buns were the best in the Midwest. She doesn't tease with him anymore, but his legs and hips still excite her. Now she feels a simmering inside, a blend of remorse and desire. She wants to slide her hand down his shorts. She wants to kiss him and confess the shame she feels about last night.

"I'm going to grab a shower," she says. "How about you? Up for a shower?"

"I don't think so. I have a million things to do."

"Like what? What's so important?"

"Who knows." Ned looks at her. His eyes are gray and stern. "You can't be like you were last night and expect things to be hunky-dory today. You want to know what's important. Healing's important. You're the doctor. You ought to know about healing."

Chase gathers up the cultivator, the sack of fertilizer, the canister of rose dust. She walks into the garage. It is cluttered with coiled hoses, garden tools, a snow blower, a lawn mower. Oil spots stain the floor. In the dimness, she stands where Rex had parked his bike. For a moment and at once he is there again peddling away: a bicycle chain rattles, the sky is blue, a dark cloud lurks. Suddenly he vanishes as if he has ridden into a rent in the earth. Chase is overcome with a sense of absence. A terrible pressure in her head. A tingling in her limbs. Tears stream down her cheeks while spears of sunlight pierce dusty air.

ALONE IN THE marriage counselor's office Chase squirms, finding her shape in a tan naugahyde chair. The walls of the office are covered with artwork that she assumes was done by children in therapy. She studies a crayon drawing of a tree, a house, and four stick figures with purple faces and no features, a smeary blue-and-red finger painting with a black sun that looks disturbed and troubles Chase. She has her pediatric patients draw pictures which she tapes to the wall in front of her examining chair during their office visits. In these pictures the characters often have enormous eyes like Little Orphan Annie. The thought of children starting out life with emotional problems saddens her.

Chase closes her eyes and tries to relax, to remember what it was like to be intimate with Ned.

Through the window, she sees the sun hanging just above the trees. The sky is a perfect pale blue. She gets up and walks to bookshelves beside a desk. She reads the titles: *Gestalt Therapy, A Clinical Guide to Menopause, How to Live (Almost) Happily with a Teenager*. She picks up a paperback, *The Man Who Danced Alone*, and thumbs through its pages. To Chase modern marriage is like modern dancing; couples no longer touching each other, writhing and jerking out of sync with the beat. She pictures herself tap dancing alone on a stage where everything is blue: the curtains, the sky in the backdrop, her taffeta gown and shoes.

The door opens, and Ned and the counselor walk in together. They are chatty and friendly. Chase is repelled by the smell of cigarette smoke on the counselor's clothing. Ned wears jeans and a plaid flannel shirt. She thinks he should have worn dress slacks and a sweater. He never dresses to fit the occasion.

At first Chase was leery of a female counselor, thinking Ned could charm her, but the counselor has gone out of her way to remain neutral. In fact everything about her is neutral: her earth tone cotton skirt and blouse, her pale face, her beige lipstick, her office with wheat walls and sand carpet. The only color in the room comes from the children's artwork. At times the counselor's neutrality annoys Chase. She wishes she would take a stand and say who is right and who is wrong.

Even if Chase is the one who is wrong, she would like to know it.

The counselor settles into a chair between Ned and Chase. She arranges her skirt, then sorts through their chart.

"Well, what about you two? How's it been going on?" She smiles hopefully.

Chase is quiet, determined to make Ned answer first for a change. The counselor looks at Ned, then she moves her gaze to Chase. She shrugs. Ned sits silently, lowering his eyes to the floor.

"How about your gardening?" the counselor asks. "Last time we talked about sharing some activities, doing something together. You mentioned gardening as something you both enjoy."

Chase likens the way the counselor probes with questions to the way Chase uses a slit lamp's beam to look through the pupil to the back of the eye with its macula and fovea centralis, the optic nerve that transmits light waves to the brain.

"Chase has her roses, I have my vegetables," Ned says. "Never the twain shall meet."

The counselor offers a tired smile. "Well, okay. I guess we need something to break the ice. If you both agree, I'd like to try a little exercise today. Sometimes it helps to open things up a bit." She searches their faces. "Does that seem okay?"

They nod.

"Here's what I want you to do. Each of you make up a story about the two of you, but don't use real people. Make it purely fictional. You could be anything—animals, creatures from another planet, cartoon characters. Whatever you want. Just let your mind go any direction it wants to."

The idea of an allegory of their marriage appeals to Chase. She is eager to excel, to show her creativity like she does when they play charades at a party. Chase is always clever while Ned hangs back inhibited.

"Got the idea?" the counselor asks. She gets up from her chair and moves toward her desk, talking as she walks. "You willing to give it a try?"

"Yes," Chase says.

"Sure," Ned replies languidly.

The counselor pulls down the blind over the desk and turns off the overhead light. The sun shining through the shade burnishes the dim room in orange. The air feels dense and brittle.

"Need to create a dream atmosphere," she says. "Now close your eyes and think about what you are. What you want to be. Relax. Let things go."

Chase closes her eyes. She hears the air conditioner's hum from outside the window, the murmur of traffic in the street. She squeezes her lids shut tighter and an aura of silver dots appear against a field of black, like blips on a radar screen. Computers. The metaphor could be computers. She and Ned could be PCs connected by a modem that transfers information back and forth between them, but they are programmed with languages that are incompatible. Next she thinks of creating a myth in which they are gods in a garden of paradise who drink a magic love potion touching off a perfect, spiritual love.

The counselor is talking now. "Do you have something? Sometimes it helps to just start and let the idea flow. Just wing it."

Chase opens her eyes. The counselor makes notes on a yellow legal pad. Chase looks at Ned. His eyes are still closed tightly, his forehead furrowed, his eyebrows bunched.

"Who's ready?" the counselor asks like a game show host. She nods at Chase. "Care to have a go at it, Chase?"

Chase hunches forward on the edge of her chair. "Okay. I'm a dog. A German shepherd. Actually, a seeing eye dog."

She imagines herself, tan and furry, black-muzzled, on a corner of a busy street. She is in a harness with Ned holding the leash. Ned is blind, his eyes cloudy, pearly-gray pools. Chase, the guide dog, pants waiting for the light to change.

"Sounds interesting," the counselor says. "Who else is in the story?"

"A blind man. He's the victim of something called retinosa pigmentosa."

Chase sees the light turn green and the dog guide the blind man through the flow of people crossing the street. The pedestrians stare at the man with his white cane and shepherd on a leash, but he is oblivious to them.

"The dog takes good care of the blind man," Chase says. "She protects him and gives him companionship, but he doesn't appreciate it. In fact, he resents it. He resents it because he wants to be independent, but that's impossible because he is blind. Sometimes he abuses the dog, transferring his frustrations and anger as if it were the animal's fault that he is blind. But the dog loves him anyway and cares for him."

Chase is beginning to enjoy making up the story. Ideas come quickly. She feels wise, as if she is exposing great truth, shedding light.

"What about the dog?" the counselor asks. "How does she react? Use an example?"

Chase searches the counselor's face, hoping for an expression of approval, but the counselor averts her gaze and jots something on her pad. Ned sits with his eyes lowered, one hand resting tensely on his knee.

An image of the guide dog, panting and straining at

her leash, focuses in Chase's mind. The dog parades down a deserted sidewalk with the man in tow. Overhead the sky is dark with churning gray clouds. The wind freshens, stirring the leaves of sycamores that line the curb. The air is charged with electricity. A metallic smell. The dog is frightened, anticipating a thunderstorm.

"The dog is leading the man to a restaurant where he is going to have lunch with his cousin and a friend. The two men are waiting for them at a table on the patio. The dog is upset because it about to storm."

Chase pictures a mossy brick patio surrounded by a boxwood hedge. White wrought-iron tables are covered by red Cinzano umbrellas, and urns of red geraniums decorate each corner. The wind blows a napkin from one of the tables. The cousin and the friend greet the blind man with handshakes.

She continues in a low monotone. "The cousin and the friend greet the blind man and ignore the dog. The cousin ties the dog's leash to a cement urn."

In her imagination, Chase hears thunder kettle-drumming, sees big raindrops bursting on brick. The dog whimpers. She is deathly afraid of lightning. The cousin leads the blind man out of the rain into the restaurant.

"It begins to rain," Chase says. "They hurry inside the restaurant and leave the dog tied up outside to get drenched. The cousin leads the blind man, but he is careless and the blind man bumps into a chair. The blind man doesn't react. If the dog had allowed that to happen, she would have been punished."

Chase is totally engrossed in the story. She doesn't think of Ned or the counselor, only the dog and the blind man. She pictures the dog, shivering and drenched, tethered in the downpour. The dog can see the blind man inside at a table, dry and warm.

Chase clears her throat and licks her lips. "The dog is left to soak in the cold rain while the blind man is inside enjoying a good meal and companionship. The dog is miserable and very angry with the blind man."

Chase pictures the three men at the table. They wash down club sandwiches and potato chips with cold beer. Everyone is laughing. Soon the rain stops, and the sky lightens.

"The rain stops," Chase continues. "The men shake hands and leave the restaurant. The dog leads the blind man toward their home, feeling cold and wet, rejected and used."

Chase stops trying to decide where to take the story. She looks at Ned. He is staring impassively at the back of his hand. Does he get it? Chase wonders.

"So," the counselor says, "we have a rejected, angry mutt. What does she do about it?"

Chase doesn't answer. She wants Ned to say

something.

"Maybe the dog doesn't do anything," the counselor says.

Chase closes her eyes and sees the dog straining at her leash, pulling the man close to the curb.

"The dog is hurt and wants to hurt back," Chase says. "She thinks of leading the man in front of an oncoming car."

"Does she?" the counselor asks.

"No."

"Why?"

"Because beneath her anger she needs the man."

"What does she need from him?" Ned asks.

"She just needs him. That's all. What's a guide dog without someone blind?"

She pauses. Her back is sweaty. Her blouse sticks to the Naugahyde chair.

"What a nice dog," Ned says. "It doesn't kill the poor guy. What does it do?"

"Well, the dog leads the man close to curb. When a car goes by, he gets splashed with muddy water from the gutter. Now the man's wet and miserable, the dog is glad, and they live unhappily ever after." Chase settles back in her chair, glancing at Ned.

"Well," the counselor says. "Good story, Chase. Much food for thought. Before we quit, I want you both to do one more thing. Give this story a happy ending. Tell me what could happen to make it turn out better."

Chase has anticipated the question, and she answers quickly. "A happy ending would be if the man had some kind of epiphany that made him see that the dog was good to him and loved him. That it wasn't the dog's fault that he was blind. That she was helping him. That he needed her."

Chase likes the sound of her words. She thinks that it's the first time since they have been seeing the counselor that she has proven her point. She is hopeful that something good will come of it.

"Is that all you want to say?" the counselor asks.

"That isn't necessarily the end," Chase says. "It could be the beginning."

"How do you mean?"

"With the man finally understanding and appreciating the dog, I see a bright future for them."

The counselor looks at her watch. She rises and walks to the window where she raises the shade. Yellow light streams through dirty panes. She turns to Ned.

"What about you, Ned? What do you think the best ending to the story would be?"

There is a long pause. Chase watches Ned shift uncomfortably in his seat. He tightens his eyebrows as if searching for a word or an idea. He says, quietly,

"Wouldn't a better ending be that the blind man regains his sight?"

Chase feels something burst inside her head. She lets out a little murmur, almost a gasp. She closes her eyes and sits in blank and empty blackness, breathing in and out. When she opens her eyes, everything is wrapped in soft dusty light. She is aware of her pupils constricting, the ciliary muscles contracting, the lens accommodating. She focuses her gaze on Ned. In his half-shadowed features, she sees the face of her son, the same dimpled chin, the same broad forehead, the same glittering gray eyes. For a moment Rex seems very near. It is as if the three of them were together again, full of love and expectations, a family.

## LEAVING LIMBO

WHEN LANCE CALLED for the first time in over a year and said he wanted to meet for dinner, I knew it wasn't about a father-son rendezvous over a good meal and a bottle of wine. It was, most certainly, an invitation for me to finance another one of his schemes, something he wanted in on or else a predicament he needed my help to escape from.

For our meeting, I had chosen Dante's, a new neighborhood Italian trattoria that had received a good review in the food section of the local newspaper. There hadn't been a decent place to eat in town since the chef left the club and ran off with the golf pro's wife, and my expectations for a good dinner were low. But anywhere would do. Lance certainly wasn't a gourmet, and although I considered myself a connoisseur of fine cuisine, I just wanted to get the ordeal behind me.

The evening of our powwow, Dante's was bustling, full of clatter and shrill laughter and the scent of too much garlic. On the walls hung posters of the leaning tower of Pisa, the Colosseum, and Ghiberti's "Gates of Paradise." The owner, a swarthy young Italian immigrant with black, oiled-back hair and an accent that reminded me of the man who once paddled my gondola around the canals of Venice, seated me at a table with a red-and-white checkered plastic cloth and paper napkins. It was near an open kitchen with a view of a wood-burning pizza oven lined with terra-cotta bricks. On my face, I could feel warmth radiating from the fire. I asked the waiter to bring me a vodka martini, Grey Goose with two ice cubes and two onions, and to replace the paper napkins with linen. As I often did in a crowd since my wife died, I felt fatigued, lonely, even a bit cold in spite of the heat from the kitchen. I tugged at the lapels of my blue blazer, glad to be wearing it and to be close to the cooking coals.

The gondolier brought me the glass of Grey Goose and the cloth napkins I requested.

"Buon appetito, Doctor," he said.

"You aren't Dante are you?" I asked jokingly.

"Did I write *The Divine Comedy*?" he said with a smile.

"No, sorry. I'm just Ugo." He unfolded a napkin and spread it on my lap. "I prefer linen myself."

"Grazie," I said. "You're a gentleman and a scholar even if you're not the bard."

I sipped the martini, savoring its bitterness. From a basket of focaccia, I broke off a piece of slightly stale bread and dipped it in a shallow dish of olive oil sprinkled with herbs and with a clove of garlic swimming in it.

When I was a boy of nine, before the days of the Salk vaccine, I was stricken with bulbar polio. The virus invaded my spinal cord and paralyzed the muscles of my throat so that I couldn't swallow. My mother kept me alive for months by feeding me liquid food through a red rubber tube that she inserted through my mouth into my stomach three times a day. I finally recovered enough to eat on my own, and eventually I became quite a healthy specimen and an excellent athlete with a six handicap and a good serve-and-volley game. But the bout of infantile paralysis did leave me with weakened swallowing muscles and a chronic dysphagia that was progressing as I aged, a condition my internist diagnosed as post-polio syndrome. I accepted this as another example of the sad reality that the older one got, the more life was filled with danger. To compensate, the lining of my throat had become hypersensitive like the fingertips of a blind person, and it was able to distinguish the texture and consistency of a bolus of food and assess whether I could swallow it without choking.

I placed the focaccia lubricated with oil in my mouth and chewed it well. When my throat told me it was ready to receive the bread, I washed it down with a big gulp of vodka. I was relieved, as often was the case, that I hadn't strangled. I tried to remember if I had ever told Lance about my bout with polio and the residual of the disease that still plagued me. I doubted that I had, because the last thing I wanted was for him to know that I was vulnerable in any way.

I looked at my steel Rolex. The bastard was already ten minutes late. Even when Lance wasn't involved, I always found myself wanting to be somewhere other than the place I was. I was ready to down my drink, settle up, and go. But where was there to go? I took another slug of vodka and held it in my mouth before I swallowed.

When the front door of the restaurant opened, I'm not sure why or what it meant, but the appearance of Lance took my breath away. Tall and fit, a striking figure with a windburned face, he was dressed in sandals and a peasant's smock-like shirt made of muslin that he had not bothered to tuck into his jeans. His hair was thinning and mussed, and the flesh under his eyes was beginning to sag. I was struck and strangely saddened by how he had ceased to be young.

The last I heard he was living in the woods some place, probably writing bad poetry, playing his flute for the squirrels, doing yoga, and meditating about who knows what. What a shame that at his age, he still hadn't found his way. For an instant he stood, looking over the restaurant as if deciding whether to enter or perhaps he was checking the female stock. "All hope abandon ye who enter here," I thought with a chuckle, remembering Dante's line from a humanities class at Vanderbilt thirty-five years ago. I kept my eyes down on the menu, hoping that if he thought I hadn't seen him, he would turn and leave. But like a monk or an apostle in the flowing sackcloth garment, he made his way toward the table where I sat with a speeding pulse. He stooped to pick up a crayon that a child had dropped on the floor. He handed it to the little boy and patted his head. I took a drink of Gray Goose and told myself to remain calm. As he came near, I was relieved to see he no longer wore an earring but was disgusted to find Chinese lettering tattooed on his forearm. Before brief careers as a social studies teacher, a flutist with a dope-infested jazz band, and then as an emergency medical technician, he had served in the Peace Corp in one of those South American countries with big-rumped señoritas, an excess of Catholics, and a left-wing government. All of that was, by the way, before his divorce from a perfectly acceptable woman with a degree from Agnes Scott. Was he now a Maoist? An opium smuggler?

"Hi, Dad," he said warily.

I thought I detected a note of guilt in his voice. If there wasn't, there should have been.

"Sir Lancelot," I said, standing. I extended my hand to ward off the embrace that I knew he didn't want either. He shook firmly as I had taught him when he was a youngster and malleable, and I was still able to influence his behavior in constructive ways. "Long time no see."

I settled back into my chair and he sat down across the table from me not bothering to place his napkin on his lap. I downed the last of my vodka, but I didn't eat the onions, fearing they might be hard to swallow.

"You didn't ride your Harley Davidson in those Jesus sandals, did you?" I asked.

Lance had no interest in my life, so it was always up to me to initiate conversation on those rare occasions when we were together.

"Indian, Dad. I've never ridden anything but Indians."

"So where's your helmet, Sir Lancelot?"

"I prefer to ride bareheaded. It's a wind-in-the-hair thing."

I had served for years on the American College of Surgeons Trauma Committee, trying unsuccessfully to get a helmet law passed for motorcyclists, and it distressed me that my own flesh and blood was one of the great unwashed who didn't see the need to protect what little brains they possessed. All I could do was shake my head.

A man in a tall white hat stoked the pizza oven in a shower of sparks.

"Don't you think it's a little warm here," Lance said, gesturing toward the kitchen. "Maybe we could move to another table."

"I like the heat," I said. "If you don't mind."

"Here's fine." He seemed to be analyzing something about me. "Are you okay, Dad? You look as if you've dropped some weight? You're not sick are you?"

"I'm fit as a fiddle. It's the Pilates I've been doing." I patted my belly. "It's taken a few pounds off. Now that I'm retired I have time for silly things like that. Nice of you to notice."

A young waitress approached the table. She was the epitome of a girl Lance would be attracted to with her little nose jewel and a ring on every finger, bleached spiky hair and that kind of low-cut blouse that loose women wear unbuttoned. She introduced herself as Star and said that she would be our server.

"Star light, star bright," Lance began almost singing the words in that honey-toned voice of his. "First star I see tonight, I wish I may, I wish I might."

The waitress blushed and let out a little laugh. I rolled my eyes at Lance. As she bent over with a pitcher to fill our water glasses, I averted my gaze from the red-and-blue star tattooed on the upper inner quadrant of her left breast.

From a handwritten menu that I could barely read in the dim light, I chose a bourgeois dinner: Caesar salad, veal marsala, and linguini with marinara sauce. I requested extra anchovies on the Caesar and fresh parmesan for the pasta. Lance ordered spaghetti and meat sauce, mispronouncing *bolognese* in the process. The wine list was pathetic, so rather than be disappointed by an overpriced domestic red, I settled on a carafe of the house Pinot Grigio. Lance ordered Budweiser in a bottle.

"Wouldn't you prefer a Peroni's in a frosted glass?" I said. "Splurge. It's my treat, as usual."

"I'm a Bud man," he said. "You know, it's the great American lager."

"Ah, that's right. And you ride an Indian *au natural*. How could I forget?" I heard the coldness in my voice and didn't regret it. "So what kind of weed are we smoking nowadays?"

"I haven't done that for years."

"Well then, this isn't about another bailout. What a relief."

"Come on, Dad. Chill out. Cut me some slack for a

change. Cut yourself some slack while you're at it."

Cut myself some slack? What was he talking about?

As we ate our salads, Lance used his left index finger to coax leaves of iceberg lettuce slathered with Thousand Island dressing onto the fork he clutched in his right hand as if it were a putty knife. When I sent him to college, where, as you might expect, he washed out of premed, I had hoped Sigma Chi would do something for his table manners, but to no avail. When he swallowed, he cleared his throat with a little grunt, an annoying habit that, unfortunately, I recognized as one of my own. He seemed nervous, and I assumed he dreaded what was to come as much as I did.

"So," he said, resting his fork on the bread plate. "Here's what I'm thinking. There's this little island off the coast of Panama."

He paused and took a deep breath. Here we go, I thought, feeling like an ATM machine. What's it going to be this time? A Buddhist sperm bank. A whorehouse for lonely dogs. He always had some altruistic pipe dream that required a major contribution from me.

"Before we get into this discussion," I said, interrupting. "I think it only right I tell you about some financial planning that's underway. It might have a bearing on the matter you're about to bring up."

He cocked his head and looked at me quizzically with his pale Siberian-husky eyes, truly startling eyes like his deceased mother's that had contributed to her remarkable beauty. And to his good looks, too, for that matter, for if he was nothing else, he certainly was good looking.

"You see," I continued on before he could comment. "I have decided to move all of my assets into a charitable remainder trust. Interest on the trust will pay me a monthly stipend to live on during my lifetime. At the time of my death the proceeds, whatever is left, will go to the charities I have designated."

I watched him turn pale. I was surprised how easily the fabrication came to me, and how authentic and full of largesse it sounded. Perhaps such a trust would be a good idea down the road.

"Who gets the money then?" he asked. "Let me guess. The symphony. The art museum. Vanderbilt, of course."

"Those sound like likely candidates."

"So, is it a done deal?" he asked.

"Nearly. My attorney is working with Fidelity on this. He tells me there should be some nice tax deductions in the offing."

I took a long drink of wine and smiled at him. Then it occurred to me that he might try to do something to me before there was time for the legal documents to be signed and he was still on the books as my only heir. But he was a passive soul, peaceful to a fault and not a threat to harm anyone but himself.

"So, that's my big plan," I said. "Now I want to hear about yours."

"You don't want hear about my crap," he said.

"No, of course I do."

At that moment, the Madonna lookalike appeared with a tray of food balanced on her bejeweled hand. I hadn't finished my salad, and I felt a little rushed but decided not to complain because I wanted to keep things moving. Star set a steaming entree on a white china plate in front of me and wished me *bon appétit* in French, not Italian, as Ugo had.

"*Merci, étoile de berger,*" I said, calling her a shepherd's evening star.

Lance rolled his eyes at me exactly as I had done to him earlier. *Touché*, I thought. These familial resemblances were as disturbing to me as they must have been to my father when he saw himself in me. The waitress served Lance his pasta, and I reminded her to bring fresh ground pepper. She obliged, revealing herself as she twisted a giant pepper mill. She retreated from the table, looking back at Lance like a she-wolf before disappearing into the kitchen. I saw the Medusa of spaghetti on his plate and imagined my head on a platter.

"The people on this island are very poor," Lance said. "And . . ."

When he acquired an idea, he was, as my grandmother used to say about me, like a hen with a chick.

"You can tell me all about your little island over dessert," I said, picking up my knife and fork. He had kept me in limbo all these years. I didn't mind seeing him spend a little time there himself. Maybe it would awaken him from the chronic slumber it seemed he was always in. "Let's enjoy our dinner now,"

"Eating mindfully," Lance said. "That's very cool, Dad, but unlike you."

The veal smothered in gravy and canned mushrooms looked for all the world like country-fried steak, but a rather pleasant meaty aroma rose from the plate. I cut off a bite and placed it in my mouth. I was surprised by how tasty and tender the morsel was, and I was eager to get on to the next bite. My caution and senses must have been dulled by the Gray Goose and Pinot Grigio, because I chewed the veal quickly and without paying heed to my dysphagia, carelessly contracted the muscles of my soft palate and pharynx. The gruel of meat started to slide down, but it abruptly stopped, lodging on my vocal cords. Oh no, I thought. I grunted and tried to cough it out, but I couldn't suck in air around the blockage and the bolus didn't budge. I tried another cough, but my airway remained obstructed. Oh, God, no. What now?

Unable to speak and not wanting to cause a scene, I rose from the table. I thought of motioning for Lance to follow me in case I needed help. But I was confident I could handle the situation myself as I could almost any medical emergency, even ruptured aortas and shattered spleens, and I had a built-in resistance to any favors he might do for me that would leave me beholden to him. So I started toward the door alone.

"Dad," Lance called.

I turned and saw him staring at me with his brow furrowed in a quizzical manner. His face glowed orange in the flames of the pizza oven.

"Are you okay?" he asked.

I mouthed, "Restroom."

With my eyes straight ahead and watering, and my napkin still tucked into my lizard belt, I quickly made my way between the tables of the crowded dining room to the entry way. As a physician, I understood the body's oxygen requirements and the ramifications of O2 deprivation. So, when I stepped out onto a deserted sidewalk, I knew that I had a few minutes to dislodge the food before hypoxia would blacken my brain and stop my heart. In the yellow gleam of a streetlight, I calmly inserted two fingers into my mouth, trying to reach down my throat to the veal, but they weren't long enough and only made me gag. I moved to the curb, telling myself to relax, but my heart was beginning to race. With one hand, I held onto a parking meter and leaned forward, first pounding my chest then thrusting my fist into my abdomen, but the meat wouldn't budge. A black Lexus sedan drove by. I waved at the passengers frantically, but the car sped on into the night. In desperation, I rapped on the restaurant's window, grasping my throat in the universal sign for choking, but no one noticed. I started to go inside, but a feeling of dizziness came over me. It was as if I were in a downward spiral and couldn't stop the fall. My panic began to ebb and my instinct for survival faded into a sort of hazy resignation. In my profession, I had often witnessed death, but for the first time, leaning against the facade of the trattoria, I was seeing death through the eyes of someone dying, and it didn't seem to matter. The moment I was about to pass out the door to the restaurant opened and Lance appeared.

"Dad," he said. "What the hell's wrong?"

Vigorously, I pointed to my neck. For a moment, Lance stood, staring at me as if he were paralyzed. I thought his time of revenge had come, and he was going to let me die. But suddenly, he grabbed my shoulders and spun me around. Then he wrapped his arms around my waist, and with balled fists delivered the blow of a Heimlich maneuver to my abdomen. But he had positioned his hands too low over my umbilicus, and his attempt failed. However, on his second try he correctly placed his fists in the epigastrium or pit of my stomach. He gave a mighty squeeze that must have cracked a rib, and the half-chewed veal shot out of my mouth and into the gutter. I fell back against Lance, coughing and sputtering, gasping for air. It was as if, unable to swim, I had fallen in deep water and had been pulled to the surface at the moment before drowning.

"Are you okay?" Lance asked, supporting me in his powerful tattooed arms.

"Yes," I managed in a raspy whisper. I released myself from Lance's grip and turned to face him. "God," I gasped. "Jesus Christ."

"Should I call ambulance? Are you going to be okay?"

"I'm fine. Just need a minute."

Lance steadied me with a hand on my elbow and led me to the entry of the adjacent Finest Footwear Shoe Store. We sat down beside each other on a concrete stoop. My throat was raw and quivering. I held my head in my hands, feeling as if I had been raised from the dead, trying to come to grips with what had happened.

Because I had conquered polio, I always believed I had earned invincibility, but in the shadowy alcove of the shoe store, a heavy net of vulnerability draped over me. Why was I so careless to allow myself to choke? When would it happen again? My own death seemed tangible, even imminent. But hadn't I already been living like a condemned man?

Lance pulled the linen napkin from my belt. He wiped my mouth and blotted sweat from the front of my shirt and the lapels of my blazer which were stained with particles of meat suspended in saliva. He placed his hand on my shoulder and looked at me. Those wolf eyes shone like pale blue pools of compassion. I didn't remember anyone ever looking at me in quite that way before. My hands were trembling.

"Breathe, Dad," he said. "Close your eyes and breathe."

I did as he said and shut my eyes. Slowly, I breathed in and out. The air that filled my lungs came in freely like a sea breeze. I could feel it deep inside my chest, pure and sweet, calming. When I opened my eyes, I saw the moon shining brightly.

# JUST WINE

WILL FIDGETED on a metal folding chair, sipping his third black coffee and wishing his cup were a glass of suitably chilled 2000 Cakebread Chardonnay. It was the doctor's first morning as a patient in Silver Lining Rehabilitation Center. He was an anesthesiologist, a handsome, graying man with the bloom of alcohol on his cheeks and a penchant for self-medication. At the country club, he was king of gin rummy, late evenings, and double malt Scotch. Now he wanted his hands to stop shaking.

"I'm Max, and I'm a recovering alcoholic," the counselor announced to the circle of problem drinkers seated in the bleak, gray-hued room.

Will studied Max's face, puffy and veined like an old boozer's, and he wondered what shape the guy's liver was in. He moved his eyes from Max to the wall. AA's Twelve Steps hung beside a poster advising to "Let Go and Let God." Fine, he thought. Then let God get me the hell out of here.

"Introduce yourselves," Max said. "Tell us why you're here, your drinking history. Say whatever comes to mind."

The patients took turns, labeling themselves alcoholics, confessing blackouts and DUIs, divorces and indebtedness, depression. Will listened, aloof. He had never been arrested; he didn't owe anyone, and his pension plan was stocked with over three million in bonds and blue chips. Who could be depressed? He tried to accept their alcoholism as a disease, not a character defect, but something inside these people with their jittery nerves and glazed expressions seemed to be broken and sagging and made it difficult to believe they weren't defectives.

"I'm Ingrid," the girl next to him said. She kept her eyes downcast. "I suppose I'm an alcoholic."

She was pretty but bone-thin and chalky with ash hair and milky skin. In a quivering voice, she confessed that she was hooked on beer and Ephedrine, trucker's speed, she called it. Her mother had been an alcoholic who committed suicide. Ingrid hit bottom the night she awakened in the sleeper seat of a semi with a man that she didn't know on top of her. She broke into tears.

"Easy does it, Ingrid," Max said. "A day at a time."

Will handed her his handkerchief. Ingrid was about the age of his daughter, Rita. So hard and hopeless. So young but already used up. Her story looped him in sadness and tugged him to the edge of tears. He wanted to put his arm around her.

It was his turn to speak. He felt everyone's eyes on him, waiting to see if he branded himself with the big A. His mouth was dry.

"I'm Will." He raised his coffee cup in a mock toast. He felt his hand trembling. He knew they could see it.

"Welcome," Max said. "Share a little about yourself. What you do. How you feel about being here."

"Well, I put people to sleep, and I'm just thrilled to be here."

Max didn't smile.

"Will's an anesthesiologist," he said. "Go on. Tell us what brings you here?"

Will pictured the intervention. His wife in tears. The chief of surgery shaking his head. The president of the hospital handing him a plane ticket to this God-forsaken place.

"Hard luck," he said.

"Good old hard luck," Max said, smiling. "We all know hard luck? Did alcohol figure into yours, Will?"

Will swirled his coffee. Max locked his eyes on him.

"You a drinker, Will?"

"Just wine. A couple of glasses with dinner. That's all. I can take it or leave it."

"The report from your hospital said nurses in the operating room smell booze on your breath and that often your words are slurred. One of your surgical patients didn't do well under anesthesia. What about that?"

Will glared at Max, but he didn't let his voice rise.

"Look," he said. "My patients do fine. I'd never do anything to jeopardize them."

"Do you read Shakespeare, Will?"

"I've read Shakespeare," Will said, trying to remember if he had.

"Then you might have heard, 'Go to your bosom. Knock there and ask your heart what it doth know.'" Max jotted some notes on a pad. "We'll leave it there for now."

He nodded toward a tall, bulky man with a head as big as a beer keg. He wore faded jeans and Hush Puppies.

"I guess we're around to you, Leon," Max said.

"Yeah, I'm Leon," the big man said. "I'm an alcoholic. Why am I here?" He hesitated a moment, selecting a piece of hard candy from a basket. "My parole officer invited me."

"Parole? You were in the joint?"

"Right, man. Twenty years stamping out license plates."

Will studied Leon. Except for a barbed-wire bracelet tattooed on his wrist, Leon didn't look like an ex-con. He appeared to be an honest, peaceful man, like a grocer or a mailman.

"What put you behind bars?" Max urged.

"Doc there would call it hard luck."

"So, what did hard luck get you?"

"Murder two."

Jesus, Will thought. He slumped in his chair. What am I doing here with these people? It was enough to make you turn to drink.

"Were you drinking, Leon?" Max asked. "Did alcohol contribute to your hard luck?"

"Sure. Booze figured in." Leon tipped his chair back and stared at the ceiling. "See it all began when me and some buddies went duck hunting. It looked like it was my lucky day. I got me a triple, three mallards, jump-shooting on this little coot pond. We had us some Schnapps. What's duck hunting without a little Schnapps? Anyhow, on the way home, we stopped at the Eagles to celebrate. We had a few, got a little crazy, started whooping it up, doing duck calls and such. One thing led to another, and it was late when I got home. I parked my pickup in the driveway and went to the door. It was locked. My wife had me locked out again."

Leon paused. He peeled cellophane from the candy and placed the candy on his tongue. His face was expressionless. Will noticed his eyes. There was no shine on them.

"So, I tell myself, Leon, it's wrong for you to be locked out of your own home. I go to my truck and get the twelve gauge. I stand on the cement stoop and pump a shell into the chamber. Then I aim at the door that's locked against me and pull the trigger." He stared at Will as if the story was for him alone. "Here's where the bad luck comes in. See, the wife was standing on the other side of that door."

The room seemed to gasp with silence. Will pictured a splintered wooden door, a woman in a nightgown sprawled in blood. A chill arced through his chest.

"Okay, thanks, Leon," Max said. He looked around the circle. "Anyone have comments on Leon's story? Is there a lesson for us?"

Will watched Leon pick bitterly at the thumbnail on his shooting hand. Will tried not to think of things. The room was silent.

"To me," Max said. "The lesson is that alcohol is the mother of hard luck."

He stood and invited everyone to join hands while they prayed the Serenity Prayer. Will bowed his head and closed his eyes. He was embarrassed by the tremor of his hand. He saw Ingrid under the trucker and Leon's wife on the floor, her body bathed in blood. Everything is luck. Nothing is luck. Will was draped in bleak desolation. He longed for the tranquility of faith. His spiritual dryness left him hollow and thirsty.

"Amen," Max murmured. "Go now but remember, what's heard here, stays here."

Will hurried into the men's rooms and locked the door. He studied his face in the mirror. He saw something abandoned, something derelict. It was there in the tarnish of his sclera, the erosions of his skin. From the pocket of his slacks, he pulled out a plastic container for contact lens solution. He unscrewed the cap and emptied the contents into his mouth. He rinsed the vodka around his teeth and tongue and swallowed it, savoring the burn in his throat. A wave of composure washed over him. He popped a breath mint into his mouth and stepped into the corridor's fluorescent light. Max was waiting for him with a cigarette in his mouth. Will kept his distance for fear Max would smell his breath.

"So," Max asked. "What did you think of your first session?"

"It was disturbing. Especially Leon's story. I feel sorry for him."

"Why so?"

"He didn't mean to kill his wife. He shot her through a closed door. Why shouldn't he get manslaughter?"

Max looked at Will, smiling as if he knew everyone's secrets, as if Will were transparent to his eyes.

"That door he shot her through, Will. It was a screen door."

Will stood for a moment aghast, crystallized with horror and wonder. He wondered if a light had been on in Leon's house. He wondered if there had been angry words between Leon and his wife. Will wondered how he let his own life become as wretched as Leon's.

# THE TRIAGE OFFICER

Triage: The allocation of treatment to battle and disaster victims according to a system of priorities designed to maximize the number of survivors.

— *The NATO Handbook of War Surgery*

ROSE AND LAVENDER AND LEMON. It all began at dawn, a pale sunrise with laminar bands of pastels bleeding beneath the clouds. In a sweat suit, I stood in the backyard admiring the horizon and sipping coffee while waiting for the caffeine to free me from drowsiness. The air was warm and still. Birds fluttered in trees and an old yellow tabby that my son, Hutch, had named Fraidy Cat, stalked a baby rabbit. In the shade of a sweet gum tree, blossoms of red rhododendrons blazed like warning lights.

The yard was dominated by a gazebo in the midst of perennial gardens near the back of the property. The old white hexagon with gingerbread trim and spindles twined with blue wisteria was once my family's haven, a little refuge from the world. Like a favorite garment, it was lovely to look at, comfortable to be in. It wrapped you in contentment. In the shade of its cedar shakes, my wife once threw pots and held ceramics classes for women in straw hats with broad brims. That was before she ran away with Margaret for an artist's life in Mexico.

In this gazebo, when Hutch was a boy, he had played doctor, slept out in his sleeping bag, and practiced the trumpet by the hour. I had listened to his laughter, his scales and triple-tonguing, and I dreamed of him growing up to become a surgeon like me—but better, more eminent, more knowing. However, Hutch, like his mother, had deserted the gazebo and me. In a recent fit of college-boy rebellion, he took his horn and moved out of the house.

There in the morning's soft light with my cooling cup of coffee, I stared at the empty gazebo, feeling a desperate loneliness. Hutch was the radiance of my life. His leaving dimmed my self-confidence and made me feel as if my luck was running out. I wished for nothing more than to have him come home for dinner. I would grill a couple of burgers with melted blue cheese and uncork a nice Merlot. The two of us would drink and chat into the night. I downed the last of my coffee.

After my daily stint on a rowing machine, a few sit-ups, and a quick shower, I drove to the hospital to make rounds. The only other surgeon in town had signed out to me for the weekend, so I had to care for his postoperative patients as well as mine. It took awhile, changing dressings and advancing drains. I reassured a guilt-stricken couple that their daughter's ruptured appendix was not their fault and that she would survive. A slender young woman on whom I had performed a mastectomy asked me what her chances were. When I told her that her lymph nodes were free of tumor and her prognosis excellent, she caught me by surprise when she got up from the bed and hugged me. I wanted to return her hug, but something held me back.

When the patients were well bedded-down for the day, I hustled home and changed into an old pair of khakis and a denim shirt. After Hutch left, being alone and idle frightened me. To distract me from loneliness, I decided to build a stone wall around a terraced rose garden that surrounded the gazebo. I laced on the olive-green jungle boots that I had worn when I was a young army surgeon in a field hospital in Chu Chi, Vietnam, during the war. With my pager clipped to my belt, I hurried to the garden. As always, when I was on call, I was tense, feeling that trouble was close at hand.

The midmorning sky was a flawless ceiling of blue bordered by a horizon that was blurred in a cloudy haze. In the shade of the gazebo, I mixed a batch of mud—three parts sand and one part Portland cement. I knelt on the ground and pounded away with my mason's hammer. Am anvil-like chink echoed through sultry air. The rhythmic sound was like a sedative, a companion. The sun roared down on my back, and soon sweat glued my shirt to my skin.

In a while, the sky shifted its mood. Blue melted into gray. A westerly breeze kicked up and a cool mist moved in, covering everything like fine mesh gauze. I quickly finished the row of stone I was laying and hurried to the garage for a sheet of plastic to cover the wall. Soon rain rattled down, and the air smelled like drenched wool.

In the kitchen, I rinsed mud off my hands and pulled a plastic bottle of Powerade from the refrigerator. I stood in the bay window guzzling the lime drink and watching big drops pelt the plastic draped over my stonework. In the quiet empty house, loneliness poured into me and pooled like water in a basin. I wondered where Hutch was and if he was safe and what his day was like.

THE LAST TIME I had seen him was two months ago. It was early in the morning, the first day of his summer break from Indiana University. When he sauntered into the kitchen, I noticed how handsome he had become. Some of his features were faintly feminine. Long dark lashes. The delicate cheek bones of his mother. His hair was tied back in a ponytail with a leather thong. He was wearing the clothes of someone released from jail: black high-top gym shoes, a black T-shirt, and stonewashed jeans with a rip in the thigh. He opened the door to the refrigerator and pulled out cartons of orange juice and milk.

I was surprised and pleased to see him out of bed so early. Usually, he racked in until noon. By the time I returned home from the hospital at night, he was off jamming with his combo. He had named the band Easy Big Fella as, I suppose, a reminder to himself, a canon to live by. Ska was the genre of rock they featured, a rollicking white man's reggae. Hutch played trumpet and sang lead. He composed most of the songs himself. "Rump Shaker." "Fruit-cup Calypso." "Surf'n the Trees." I liked his music. The lyrics were typical of Hutch— joyous and nonsensical with "doo-wah-diddys" and "gabba gabba goos." His ballads were moving and tender, maybe a little sentimental.

"Well," I said. "Look what the cat drug in."

"Hey, Pop."

He came to the table and leaned over and hugged me. I liked to be hugged by him. My father and I never hugged.

"Great to have you home," I said.

He stood, shaking cereal from a box into a blue bowl. I was disappointed to see he was getting a little paunch. I assumed it was from all the beer he was drinking in the Bloomington bars where he performed. But how could I be critical? He was a premed who had just made the Dean's list for the fifth semester in a row, setting the curve in organic chemistry. He brought the bowl of breakfast food to the table and settled onto the cane seat of a chair across from me. He poured on the milk and heaped the cereal with brown sugar.

Hutch folded open a Rand McNally road atlas. While he studied a map of the United States, he used his index finger to tap out a rhythm on the table, the beat, I supposed, of one those little tunes that he was always composing in his head.

"Going somewhere?" I asked.

"West," he said sheepishly, his voice still husky from sleep and cigarettes. "Seattle."

"Hope you like rain. What are you going to do there?"

"Get a job. I'm planning to pursue my dream of becoming a professional sports team mascot," he deadpanned.

I smiled, picturing him in the costume of the San Diego Padres' chicken.

"Actually, we're taking the band to Seattle," he said. "Ska is huge out there. It's the place for us to be."

"So, what about medical school?"

Hutch took a long drink of orange juice from the carton. He looked at me with dark, serious eyes.

"I've decided not to go. I'm not cut out for medicine, Dad."

I took another swallow of coffee, trying to calm myself.

"You're just burned out," I said. "Take a semester off. Take your trip west. Then come back with your battery recharged."

"Dad, I can't see myself as a doctor."

"What do you see yourself as?"

"I don't know. A musician, I guess. I'm searching." He dabbled with his spoon in the bowl of cereal. "Remember last summer when I worked as orderly? I was afraid to talk to you about it, but it made me realize medicine wasn't for me."

"Why?" I asked. "Everyone was complimentary about the way you handled yourself."

"I don't know. Being around all those people dying with cancer and stuff. I felt sad all the time. I couldn't spend my life like that."

"That's something you learn to deal with," I said. "You learn to put your feelings aside."

"See. That's the point. I don't want to have to put my feelings aside. I want to express them. With music, I can."

"Wait a goddamn minute," I said. "You're saying rock and roll is somehow emotionally superior to medicine? Give me a break."

"I'm just saying how I feel."

Heat boiled up the back of my neck. I glared at him.

"You and all your high and mighty feelings. You know, you're like all the other goddamned doctors' kids in town. You're not hungry. Everything's been laid out on a silver platter for you. You don't know what it's like to go after something with everything you've got."

"You don't know me," he said. "You don't understand."

"What is it I don't understand? Let me tell you one thing . . ."

"Save it," he said. "Just save it."

He stormed out of the kitchen. I dumped my coffee cup in the sink and moved heavily outside. I sat on the steps of the gazebo, staring off in the distance. Before long, Hutch stepped out of the house, letting the door bang closed behind him. He wore an old felt fedora with the brim turned up and a feather stuck in the band. Under one arm, he cradled a duffel bag. His other hand was hooked around the handle of his trumpet case. With the cat trotting beside him, he lugged the gear to his Jeep. He tossed the duffel bag in the back and eased the horn onto the passenger seat.

"Where do you think you're going?" I asked.

"Somewhere. Anywhere."

He leaned over and stroked Fraidy's fur. Then he straightened up. He opened the Jeep's door and folded himself onto the seat. He craned his head out the window and our eyes locked. We stared at each other for what seemed like a long time, but what must have been only a second or two. It was a moment that would determine our fate, a moment when, with a few words from me, a different outcome may have been possible. He turned his head away and the Jeep roared down the driveway, its tires scattering gravel. For a while I sat looking out into the road.

Now with my Saturday's plans to build a wall dissolving in the downpour, I thought of calling around to find out where Hutch was, but I chose to leave him alone and let him learn a lesson. He needed to get a little hungry, a little poor. I decided to ride over to Hap's Homebuilder and pick up a couple bags of Portland cement.

In my Blazer, I crossed a suspension bridge over the Blue River, a wide stream with steep gray banks of layered limestone. The cars coming toward me had their headlights on. Their tires left a wake of fine spray. From somewhere in the distance came the cry of sirens. I drove on through rain that came in deepening shades of green. Just when I spotted the Hap's sign, the pager on my belt beeped shrill staccato notes that injected me with a little dose of adrenalin. I glanced down at the number on the pager's lighted screen. It was 777, the hospital's emergency room. My heart jumped.

I wheeled the Blazer around the gas pumps of the Big Foot convenience store and headed east toward the hospital. I could easily have been a plastic surgeon with regular hours, a plush office, and a big income. But there was something about trauma surgery that filled me with excitement and secret pleasure. It was the same thing that made men want to be rock climbers instead of fly fishermen. To the beat of windshield wipers, I speeded on.

In the distance, the smokestack of the hospital's power plant loomed against a sky of tumbling charcoal clouds. The sirens had silenced, and I heard the rain drumming on the Blazer's metal skin. I turned into the parking lot. The asphalt shimmered and swam like a black lagoon. My mind was on alert, my senses like a hunter's at dawn.

Under the ER's brick-pillared porte cochère, three ambulances were parked with their motors idling, the exhaust pipes steaming. There was something ominous about their empty cargo holds and the warning flashers spinning red through the rain. I sprinted in downpour, knowing I was soon going to be in the middle of something. What was I rushing toward? A shattered liver. A splintered spleen. A ruptured aorta. At times, trauma surgery is like climbing a mountain and finding yourself on a sheer, terrifying rock-face.

The ER's doors swung open. With my heart whomping, I burst into a cacophony of shattered light and noise. A nurse shouted for help. A telephone rang unanswered. An orderly in scrubs sprinted by me. I heard a scream. For an instant, I was back at the field hospital in Nam with a chopper landing, medics with a stretcher sprinting through swirling red dust. A nurse dropped a bottle of saline and it shattered on the tile floor.

"What the hell we got?" I asked a deputy sheriff in a yellow slicker.

"Big crunch," he said. "A head-on. It's bad, man. One dead at the scene. We got two in here that's critical. You're going to need some help, Doc."

My muscles tightened.

"I'm it," I said. "I'm the Lone Ranger."

From behind the curtain of the shock room, a slim nurse with scattered red hair leaned out. Blood stained her white smock. She was Rosemary, a pretty divorcée who lived in a little Cape Cod near me. She invited me over now and then for champagne and croquet. Frantically, she flagged me toward her.

"In here," she yelled.

I moved toward her, grabbing a stethoscope from the counter of the nurse's station.

"Hurry," she said.

"What you got?"

"Two boys in shock. One's in coma with a closed head injury."

Her voice quivered. Rosemary was an old trauma veteran, cool under pressure. She could start an IV in the eye of a hurricane. I had never seen her panicked before. As I started into the cubical, she gripped my arm.

"The boy in here," she said. "It's Hutch."

"Oh, God. No."

My heart battered my chest wall. I pushed past Rosemary into the shock room. The floor was littered with bloody gauze, a snarl of plastic tubing, and a rain-soaked felt fedora. Hutch was sprawled on a gurney. His shirt and jeans had been cut away, leaving him naked except for his black, high-top tennis shoes. Blood trickled from his ear. Dark bruises surrounded his eyes. I held his face with my hands, being careful not to move his neck.

"Hutch! Hutch! Can you hear me? It's Dad."

Saliva gurgled from his mouth.

I checked his pupils with a pen light. They were dilated and fixed, black like lumps of obsidian.

"Hutch," I pleaded. "Wake up, Son." I pressed my knuckles hard against his sternum, trying to arouse a response to pain. "Say something, Hutch."

His mouth blew a bubble of spit. I had to look away. I turned to Rosemary. "What's he been like?" I asked. "Did he respond when he came in?"

"He's been totally unresponsive. I'm pumping in fluids, but I can't keep his pressure up."

I probed his belly with my fingers, seeking the source of his shock. His abdomen was taught and distended with a purple band across his umbilicus where a seat belt had bruised him. My heart was churning, my hands shaking. I knew his peritoneum was full of blood. Rosemary wiped the saliva from his face with a washcloth.

"Your Dad's here," she said. "He's going to take care of you."

I smoothed my hand across Hutch's forehead, brushing his hair back.

"I'm here, Hutch," I said. I sucked in a long breath and fought off tears. "Just hang in there."

I stepped back from the gurney. The floor seemed to dip and sway. I braced myself, trying to calm down and think clearly. It occurred to me that if I could get him to surgery and stop the bleeding in his belly, then we would lifeline him by helicopter to a neurosurgeon in

Indianapolis who could treat his brain injury. I turned to Rosemary and started to tell her to call the OR when Bea Sims, a heavyset Black nurse in blue scrubs, tore through the cubicle curtains.

"I need you stat," she said. "The kid in Trauma 2's going sour."

I glanced down at Hutch. In his state of dark unconsciousness, his arms and legs had stiffened into an ominous, brainless posture known as decerebrate rigidity.

"Get a unit of packed cells going," I yelled to Rosemary as I backed out of the cubical. "Pump it in. Have four more available. Tell the OR to get ready. I'll need my vascular instruments."

I dashed into the adjacent trauma cubical. On a gurney, a bony boy with a shaved head writhed and moaned. His face was pale as paste. He wore a diamond stud in his ear. On his neck, a blue star had been tattooed. I recognized him as Ray Lopez, the drummer for Easy Big Fella. He came from the Island, a ragged part of town around the tomato canning factory. He had been a tough little halfback on Hutch's football team in high school. I always admired Ray's spunk. But he was a hustler with a reputation for drugs. I was never comfortable with Hutch hanging around him. I picked up Ray's wrist. His skin was cold and waxen, his pulse a faint peck against my fingers. I examined him rapidly, auscultating his chest, tapping out his reflexes, palpating his limbs for fractures. Everything seemed normal. I pressed my hand into his abdomen. It was distended with a seatbelt's bruise—same as Hutch's. The way Lopez screamed and tensed his rectus muscles told me he, too, was bleeding into his belly. Ray looked at me with wild, dark eyes.

"Don't let me die," he pleaded, half out of his head.

I moved away from him into corridor between the two trauma cubicles. The ER grew strangely quiet. The nurses, the EMTs, the orderlies, everyone seemed to have their eyes on me.

In Vietnam, I had learned the art of triage. Dust-off helicopters choppered the wounded to Chu Chi, ten, sometimes fifteen, at once. There was a little alcove behind a screen in the field hospital's holding area where the most experienced surgeon, the triage officer, banished the GIs who had the least hope of survival while we operated on those who had the best chance to live. It didn't matter who anyone was or what they had done. Rank had no privilege. Emotions didn't matter. It was pure Darwinism. Perpetuation of the species. Survival of the fittest.

I peered in at Hutch, my son, the repository of my hope and love. His black tennis shoes stuck out over the end of the stretcher—a boy who had outgrown his bed. Blood streamed from a plastic bag into his IV tubing. He lay motionless, his eyes fixed on the ceiling light like a drowned man's eyes on the sun. Even if I could save him, what would I be saving him for? A life of hell. A vegetative existence in a nursing home. But I'd read case reports of patients with brain injuries who had eventually awakened from their comas and returned to life. The printout on the monitor said his systolic blood pressure had dropped to 60. I felt as if my heart would explode.

"Oh fuck. I'm going to die!" Ray Lopez cried out again. "Please don't let me die."

I swung my gaze away from Hutch toward Ray. With his shaved head and in the fetal position, he looked embryonic. I wished that his heart would stop. I wished that Hutch would rise up from the gurney and call to me. The mechanical doors that lead to the surgery suite hissed open, and Joe, an old orderly from the OR, appeared. He wore green scrubs and a paper beret. On his forearm was a tattoo of a snarling tiger.

"OR's ready," he wheezed, short of breath. "Who goes?"

"In here, Joe," Rosemary called. She pulled the sheet up to cover Hutch's nakedness. His face was as white as the sheet. I watched the rhythmic rise and fall of his chest. My own respirations had synchronized with his as if he were deep within me, breathing. With a kick, Rosemary released the footbrake on the gurney and started to push Hutch toward the operating room. My heart raced. My legs trembled. I grabbed the cart's chrome rail.

"Stop!" I said. "We have two patients here."

"For Godssake," Rosemary said. "This is Hutch."

"Just wait," I said.

My mind swirled, searching for a reason to choose Hutch. I started to announce that Ray Lopez might have an injury to the great vessels in his chest. Before I could take him to the operating room, he needed a CAT scan to rule out a rupture of the aorta. It was Hutch who should go to surgery. No one could challenge my decision. I was the triage officer.

Lopez's scream tore through the stillness. I turned and watched him struggle to a sitting position.

"Don't let me die," he pleaded.

Then he howled like the dying animal he was, and I wanted to howl, too. I stepped across the corridor into his cubical and took him by the shoulder.

"You're not going to die, Ray," I said. "Lie down."

I sucked in a deep breath and let it out slowly. Then I turned to Rosemary.

"Let's go," I said. "Get Lopez to the OR. Stat."

I didn't look at Hutch again.

GOWNED AND GLOVED under the operating room's hot white lights, I felt as if I were hallucinating. It was as if the wet warm belly my hands were swimming through was a tactile mirage. Ray Lopez's spleen had been lacerated. A jagged star-shaped rent on its lower pole spewed a stream of dark blood into his peritoneal cavity. I controlled the flow with pressure on the wound from the fingers of my left hand. I swept my right hand behind the spleen, breaking up filmy attachments to the silky muscle of the diaphragm. The spleen came free, and I cradled the spongy organ in my grasp. The livid red capsule glistened in the light. Instantly, the operative field was drenched with blood. I knew I had torn one of the flimsy arteries that supplied the spleen. For a moment, I froze, watching the vessel spurt. I thought of doing nothing to control the bleeding. If I let Ray Lopez die, I could get to Hutch.

"Hemostat," I barked at the scrub nurse. "Suck, goddamn it. I can't see shit."

She slapped the instrument into my gloved hand. I dove the hemostat into a puddle of blood and closed its jaws. Immediately the bleeding stopped.

"Hemostat. Come on. Keep them coming."

I worked across the splenic hilum, systematically clamping the vessels twice, cutting between the clamps with a Mayo scissors, and tying off the bleeders with ligatures of black silk. I was all reflexes, operating in a trance.

With the spleen in a stainless steel pan and the bleeding controlled, I took a deep breath and bent over to allow the circulating nurse to mop my brow with a towel. I glanced through the window above Sam Miller, the anesthesiologist. The rain had stopped, and a patch of blue shone through a crack in the pale white sky. I thought it might be a sign that Hutch was alive, that the bleeding in his belly had tamponaded, that the edema of his brain had miraculously melted away and he was awake. For a moment, hope arose in me.

Suddenly, Rosemary appeared in the door. My heart leapt and lodged in my throat. She hadn't bothered to wear a mask or gown, and I knew my hope must be nothing more than a dirty trick. For an instant our gazes locked. Then she looked away and whispered something to Sam Miller. He shook his head. Rosemary left, and the operating room was silent except for the wheeze and sigh of the ventilator. A monitor's mournful beep. The scrub nurse handed me a needle holder loaded with suture. I began to close the abdomen, taking deep bites in the fascia of the rectus muscles and tying the monofilament with one-handed surgeon's knots. I didn't think I had the strength to finish, but I kept telling myself, "Go on. You have to do this. You have to go on."

After I clipped the last staple into Ray's skin, I

backed away from the table. I peeled off my bloody gloves and tossed them in a plastic bag. Sam turned off a dial on his gas machine. Over his mask, his eyes were blue pools of sadness.

"My boy?" I asked.

Sam took my arm in his hand and held it tightly, but he wouldn't look at me.

"He's gone," he said.

Something ruptured inside me, and my strength drained away. I felt as if I couldn't breathe. I fought to keep from dropping to my knees and pounding the ground with my fists. I shucked my gown and let it fall. In the corridor, I sank down on the terrazzo floor, quivering. In a trance, I wondered about all the music that had been inside Hutch and where it was now. With my back against the wall, I wept.

AFTER HUTCH'S MEMORIAL SERVICE, his mother and I spread his ashes on a pond I owned in the hills and forests of southern Indiana. The acreage was a serene wilderness that Hutch loved and where we fished for blue gill and picnicked as a family.

For a while, I tried to live stoically and get through each day, hoping life would somehow return to something worth living. I hated to hear people talk about their children. Not many of my friends came to see me. Those who did didn't know how to act around me, and I never knew what to say to them. I continued to practice surgery, masquerading as a contented man, but I was only an impersonator of my former self. The patient's pain added to my own pain and made it harder to bear.

When I went home at night to the vast empty house, the essence of Hutch lingered in the shadows of all the rooms. The stereo speakers, the photographs, the baby grand piano, every object seemed to announce that he was gone. Memories of him were like reflections in a room of mirrors. Memories reflecting memories of memories. The images of Hutch continually came to me in brilliant detail. The felt hat with the feather that he wore when he left that day. The way he swung his hips when he sang "Rump Shaker." The way he asked when he was a little boy, "Daddy, can I do it all by myself?" These memories haunted me, filled me with dread and regret. For a while I talked into a tape recorder every night to feel as if I were talking to Hutch, telling him about my day. But nothing worked, nothing made life seem worthwhile. It was as if my soul had left my body. I was like the Indian who cut his own throat in Hemingway's "Indian Camp" because: "He couldn't stand things."

Finally, I quit practice. I sold the big Victorian home with the gazebo and gardens and ghosts. On a hill overlooking the pond where Hutch's ashes were cast, I built a simple cabin with 150-year-old poplar logs and cherry wood floors. I settled there to be near the sky.

As time passed, living an elemental life close to the earth and its cycles transformed and restored me, refilled the hollow where my soul once was. I slowly came to accept the fact that life and death are Siamese twins, two faces of one reality.

Now I am old but not unhappy. I'm certain I am where I should be at this time in my life. I have grown a beard, and my hair is long and white. I tie it back in a ponytail with Hutch's leather thong. I love to walk alone on the paths I have made through tall hardwoods, moss and mushrooms at my feet. My sorrow and despair vanish the way the shadows of the trees disappear in sunlight. I read the mystics, Buddhist poets, and Thomas Merton. I listen to opera and bluegrass music. I build stone walls and cairns to mark the trails. I cut wood for the stove that heats my cabin. That's the only triaging I do, thinning aging oaks and dying beeches to allow young maples and walnuts to flourish.

I have learned to play a mahogany hammered dulcimer, not with the virtuosity Hutch played the trumpet, but competently. Now and then I get together for a little picking and fiddling with a violinist and guitarist, an elderly couple, who live up the road. The dulcimer's haunting, tinny tones sustain themselves and comfort me. Like Hutch once said about himself, my feelings speak through the music.

At twilight on most evenings, you will find me in a swing on my front porch, sipping a Manhattan and watching the sky over the trees deepen in shade and hue. Sometimes I close my eyes and hum one of Hutch's tunes, hearing only the music of the moment. Other times I might contemplate a leaf floating down onto the water, knowing that I will see the leaf again very soon. When darkness settles in and whippoorwills begin their song, often a deer steals out of the woods to lick a block of salt on the pond's shore. From the porch, I can't see him, but I know Hutch is there. I can hear him moving in the trees.

# WIDOW'S WALK

DUSK WAS my favorite time of the day. Most evenings after work at the island clinic, I changed into walking shorts, sandals, and a polo shirt, and with a big tumbler of Chardonnay, went alone to the beach to enjoy the sunset. With the changing shapes of clouds and shades of lavender and orange that streaked above the water like the brush strokes of an abstract expressionist, the sky was never the same but always pastel and beautiful. For an hour or so, the day's last light allowed me to escape my loneliness and feel less hopeless.

One evening when a warm wind blew out of the south and surf burst on the shore, splashing up spray and spume, I saw a woman walking toward me on the beach. For an instant, I was startled, thinking she was Diana, my dead wife. As the woman drew nearer, I could see that she was tall and attractive, dressed in yellow toreador slacks and a flowered top with spaghetti straps. I sipped my wine and watched her throw a tennis ball into the waves for a black Labrador retriever to fetch. I was fifty-eight, and I estimated her to be about ten years younger. I liked her athletic build: the long legs and slender hips, the sinewy arms and pert breasts, the sporty way she wore a baseball cap with a blond ponytail streaming from beneath it. I could tell she was someone of privilege, as were most of the women who wintered on the island.

When I was an undergraduate at Williams, I had majored in both premed and English literature. I read the great physician authors: Walker Percy, William Carlos Williams, Somerset Maugham, and my favorite, Chekhov. The woman brought to mind Chekhov's "The Lady with the Dog." In a moment of fantasy, the sandy strip of beach with its shells and dunes of sea oats became the esplanade in Yalta, and I was Dmitri Dmitritch Gurov, the woman my lover, Anna Sergeyevna.

The imaginary Anna took the tennis ball from the mouth the dripping animal, then stroked its back while the dog nuzzled her leg. I thought she must be kind and loving. But there was something about the way she moved, a languidness that made me suspect she, too, was troubled. Who are you? I wondered. Where are you staying? Are you married? Why are you sad?

Without looking toward me, she continued on down the beach with the dog frolicking along the water's edge and barking at sandpipers. I followed her from a distance, pausing occasionally to pick up a shark's tooth and have a sip of wine. At Trail's End, an old, rambling Florida-style cottage with a metal roof and a widow's walk, she and her dog climbed the steps of a concrete breakwater. She washed sand from her feet and the Lab's paws with a stream of water from a hose. Then they disappeared into the cottage. The screen door closed behind her with a bang. I turned toward the water just in time to see the sun slip below the horizon, leaving the sky pink over an ocean that seemed like a vast and dune-less desert.

THAT NIGHT, algae bloomed off the shore, coating the water with a reddish-brown sheen and enveloping the island in an invisible cloud of caustic fumes. In the days that followed, this red tide drove all the sunbathers and surf casters, coughing and sneezing, from the beach. A mother manatee and her pup were found floating in a bayou, killed by the algae's toxin. Dead mackerel, snook, and a giant grouper were washed onto the beach. Seagulls pecked at fishes' eyes and stinking carcasses.

In spite of the astringent air that stung my eyes and

made my tongue and lips tingle, I continued to go to the beach at sunset with white wine and expectations. But the woman and her dog never appeared. A feeling that my future was without possibility returned to me. I rationalized her disappearance by telling myself I had been spared another relationship, like my marriage, that was doomed to end in heartbreak and loss.

Two days later during the night, the wind shifted to the east. When I awakened in the morning, the red tide was gone, the water placid and green. The island's air was clean and sweet again with the scent of jasmine and bougainvillea. At sunset that evening, from my screened-in porch, I spotted the woman and her dog far down the beach. She was wearing a one-piece black bathing suit. In her hand was a tennis racquet that she used to serve a ball into the water for the dog to retrieve. At the sight of her, my heart sped. I hurried to the water's edge. I picked up a whelk and examined it as if I were collecting shells. Soon the black Lab, a red bandanna tied around its neck, trotted to me. It wagged its tail. I reached out and scratched the dog's head.

"Hello, beautiful," I said as if to the dog but meaning its master who was still a distance away.

I took the tennis ball from the dog's mouth and threw it into the water. The Lab swam out and brought it to me, dousing me with a salty spray that it shook from its fur.

"Lilly," the woman commanded, drawing near. "Calm down." She bent over and held the dog by its collar. "I'm sorry. She gets excited."

"Lilly's fine," I said, smiling. I threw the ball as far as I could into the surf. "Go get it, Lilly."

She released Lilly, and the dog splashed into the water. I turned to the woman. For the first time, I was able to study her at close range. Her hair was a dry and sun-faded blond, her face lightly freckled. From the corner of her eyes, which were pale blue and flecked with brown, radiated creases of age and worry. She appeared plainer and older than I had first thought, but somehow this made her even more attractive. I was disappointed to see a gold wedding band on her finger.

"Hasn't this red tide been something?" I asked.

"Frightful," she said. "What in the world causes it?"

"There's a bloom out in the gulf," I said. "A species named *Gymnodinium breve* to be exact. It gives off a toxin that's quite irritating to mucous membranes. We see a lot people at the clinic who think they have bronchitis or pneumonia, but it's just the red tide."

"You must be a doctor," she said.

"Yes," I said. "I'm retired and work at the clinic part time."

"It must be nice to be a doctor in paradise," she said.

"It has its moments."

Lilly pranced in front of me, wanting to play. I took

the ball from her mouth and threw it into the water again.

"Here for the season?" I asked.

"I don't know," she said. "Everything's a little uncertain right now."

The melancholy in her voice, the weariness in her eyes, made me wonder.

For a while, we stood, watching the dog and the yellow circle of sun that hung above the water like a Calder mobile. I told her my name, and she introduced herself as Judy. Like Anna and Dmitri in Chekov's story, we talked for a while, discussing the pattern of clouds and the trick of light that sometimes results in a green flash the instant after the sun drops below the horizon. She asked me what my specialty had been. I told her it was surgery and that working at the clinic gave me a way to keep my hand in medicine without all the stress and responsibility of the operating room. I admitted that at times I felt a little guilty about being a missionary to the rich, but I acknowledged that even the wealthy had their needs.

"That I can attest to," she said in a way that me think she was referring to herself.

I was curious to know why she considered herself needy.

Judy told me that her father had been a doctor and that she trained Labs and golden retrievers to become canine companions for the disabled. Lilly was one her students that didn't qualify. That she failed to mention her marriage gave me encouragement.

"Could I interest you in a glass of Chardonnay?" I asked. "I have nice bottle chilling in the house."

"Thanks," she said. "I'd love a glass, but I need to get home." She swung her eyes from the sun to the dog at her feet. "Come on, Lilly girl."

"Wait," I said. "There may be a green flash, and you'll miss it."

"Have you ever seen it?"

"No. But tonight may be the night. They say it has to be hot with no clouds. All the atmospheric conditions are just right."

"I really must be getting back. But thanks anyhow."

I watched her as she moved away down the beach with the dog at her side. After she disappeared into Trail's End, I turned and looked out to sea I watched the sun on its lonely descent, wondering, desiring. From a distance came the piercing cry of an osprey. Suddenly the orange orb dropped from sight. No green flashed in the sky.

THE NEXT MORNING when I stepped from my paneled office into the corridor of the clinic, Judy was standing at the nurse's desk with a patient's history form. The sight of her in linen shorts and a pale blue polo shirt caused a prickling sensation to come over me. I buttoned my white lab coat and brushed back my hair to cover my baldness. Then I approached her.

"Well," I said, cheerfully, "what brings you in today? The red tide's gone. It can't be that."

"I'm not the patient," she said. "You're seeing my husband." Her expression was grim. She handed me the history form. "This will tell you about him."

Judy turned and stepped into the examining room. For a few minutes, I studied her husband's medical history. His name was Charles, his age sixty-three. He was a banker from Cincinnati, Ohio. His diagnosis was colon cancer with metastasis. Previous surgery included a colon resection with a colostomy. He had been treated with 5 FU chemotherapy.

I thought for moment, then I entered the room. Slumped on the end of the examining table was Charles, tall and gaunt in a blue velour sweatsuit and house slippers. The skin of his face and neck was slack and gray. His pallid cheeks were stubbled. There were dark hollows above his collarbones and around his rheumy eyes. Sunken and shadowed, he was the very picture of malignancy. A man with no future, I thought. Nothing but a statue of dust.

I introduced myself and shook his hand. His skin was

cadaveric, and an odor like rotting wood hung in the air around him.

"I've seen you on the beach," Charles said, laboring to breathe.

I knew for me to help him, he had to trust me. I hoped I hadn't done anything to jeopardize that.

"From Trail's End," I said. "My favorite house on the island."

"It's aptly named," he said.

I looked down at his chart to avoid his gaze.

"I know about your history of colon cancer," I said, "Tell me how I can help you today."

"The pain," he said. "It's getting unbearable."

"On a scale of one to ten how would you rate your pain?"

"Eleven," he said. "It's like a damn knife sticking in my side."

"What are you taking for it?"

"Vicodin." He lifted his watery blue eyes to me like a beggar. "I need something stronger. I can't take it."

"Lie back and let me check you," I said. "Then we'll see what we can do to make things better."

I glanced at Judy, who was watching us from a chair. Her face was expressionless. When I lifted Charles's shirt, I saw that his belly was roadmapped with surgical scars, the skin scalded from radiation. Scraping with my fingernails, I peeled a plastic bag from his colostomy.

The moist, pink bloom of bowel gurgled and erupted something like wet mud. The small room smelled like a porta-potty. My saliva turned bitter. I felt nausea in the back of my throat. Seeing the horrible situation the man was in, I was ashamed of my own self-pity. I looked at Judy again, and she lowered her eyes. I pressed my hand into Charles's doughy abdomen. On the surface of the liver, my fingertips found big tumor nodules hard as stones.

"Your appetite," I asked. "How is it?"

He wrinkled his nose in disgust.

"He picks at his food like a sparrow," Judy said. "He was always such a big eater. He hasn't eaten in days. Tell him he should eat."

"Why should I eat?" he asked, before I could say anything.

I searched for words of hopefulness that I could convey, but nothing true came to mind.

"You're on chemotherapy," I said. "You need calories to fight your tumor."

"I stopped chemotherapy before we came down. All it was doing was making me puke. There was no point."

I gave Charles's shoulder a little pat.

"You can sit up now," I said.

"Just a minute," Judy said.

She stepped to the table. From a paper sack, she

plucked a pair of disposable rubber gloves, a packet of Kleenex, and a plastic colostomy bag.

"The nurse can do that," I said.

"He wants me to do it. I know how it goes."

With a tissue she cleansed him, carefully blotting his raw skin, dabbing at the bowel. I watched the movement of her hands as she fit the bag around the stoma. She did it gently. Her tenderness stirred a longing in me. When she pressed with her fingers to seal the adhesive to the skin, Charles groaned.

"Sorry, Dear," she said.

"I know you are."

Slowly, painfully, Charles pried himself from the table and sat hunched forward with his head bowed, staring at the floor. Maybe he wants to talk, I told myself. Don't hurry. Let him talk. Listen to him. I took my time, pulling a metal stool beside him and settling onto it.

"So how are your spirits holding up?" I asked.

"Sometimes I get really down," he said in a raspy voice. "Way down."

"How do you handle it?" I asked. "What gives you pleasure?"

"I like to sit up on the widow's walk and look out at the sea. Watch an osprey or a pelican dive. See the dolphins." He nodded toward a watercolor that hung on the wall. It was a painting of a fisherman in a wooden boat with the tarpon on his line breaking water. "I used to love to fish like that." He paused to catch his breath and look at Judy. "Sometimes she'll join me, and we talk. We don't talk about how I feel, or my cancer. We just talk about small things. Our children. The trips we took. Things like that."

I don't know how you can envy a dying man, but listening to Charles, I envied him.

"I get tired easily and have to lie down," he continued. "She gives me a back rub with baby oil. If I'm lucky, I'll fall asleep for a while."

For a moment in my mind, it was my back Judy was rubbing with oil. I glanced at her. Her eyes were closed as if to hide tears. A liquid ache flowed under my skin. I swallowed hard.

"That back rub," I said. "It must feel good."

"How about my pain?" Charles said. "What are we going to do about that?"

"We can handle it. There's no reason for you to be in pain. I'm going to start you on liquid morphine." I noticed how blue his lips were. "I'm going to order some oxygen to ease your breathing." I rose from the stool and started for the door. "I'll write a couple of prescriptions and arrange for oxygen."

"My surgeon up north talks to me with his hand on the doorknob," Charles said. "Thanks for listening without your hand on the knob."

I gave a little smile and nodded.

"I'm available if you need anything. There's no reason for you to suffer. Don't hesitate to call me. I'm right down the beach."

At the nurse's station, I stood, writing the prescription for liquid morphine sulfate, 4 milligrams every two hours as needed. I thought what a wonderful drug morphine was, the way it eased pain and breathing and put worry to rest, the kindness it could bestow. If I could have only one drug to use for my patients, I would want it to be morphine. Judy stepped out of the examining room. She closed the door behind her and came to me.

"What do think about him?" she asked in a near whisper.

"He's very sick."

"How much longer is this going to go on?" she asked.

My years in medicine had taught me how unpredictable death was, how cruel it could be by making you wait.

"It's impossible to know," I said. "There's a lot of tumor. I doubt that he has long." I handed her the prescription. "There are some rough days ahead. Maybe you should take him home to Ohio while he can still travel." I said it, but I didn't want her to leave the island.

"No," Judy said. "He wants to die here. That's why we came. His father brought him here to fish for tarpon when he was a boy. He wants his ashes scattered in the pass when the tarpon are rolling."

"How about you?" I asked. "How are you holding up?"

"You do what you have to do." She held up the prescription for morphine. "What happens if he gets too much of this?"

"He quits breathing. But don't be afraid of it. Give him what he needs." I was thinking that an overdose would be a kindness. Was that what she was considering? "Call me if you need something. We can arrange for Hospice to be involved. I can come by the house and see him. I'm always available."

"I'm okay for now. You've been very kind."

I watched her go back into the examining room. At the door, she turned and looked at me. I smiled, thinking what a magnificent woman she was.

IN THE TWO days that followed, I continued my sundown stroll by Trail's End. With a sense of anticipation I hadn't felt in years, I searched the house and yard, hoping to see Judy, but the windows were always dark, the widow's walk deserted. I called a couple of times, but no one answered. I assumed they had changed their minds and returned to Ohio. I believed I would never see her again. I had that empty feeling one gets when he feels opportunity is lost.

However, the next evening at sunset, Judy appeared on the breakwater with Lilly at her side. She was barefoot and dressed in a white cotton peasant dress. When I saw her, my heart sped. I walked over to her and petted the dog.

"How's Charles doing?" I asked.

She closed her eyes and shook her head. Her face without makeup was very pale.

"He's gone," she said. "It happened last night."

"I'm so sorry," I said.

"I'm glad it's over for him," she said. "I feel a great sense of relief."

"I hope he was comfortable," I said.

"Your medicine worked wonders. He was grateful to you."

"I could tell you took good care of him," I said. "You can feel good about that."

"He was a good man," she said. "He deserved it."

I thought that to be called a "good man" was the best obituary someone could have. If it was true, then nothing else mattered.

Judy started down the steps. She seemed unsteady, and I took her hand to help her. The dog trailed with its head down, slumped in mourning. We walked slowly to the water's edge. We stood in the sand with Lilly at

Judy's feet. Waves lapped at the shore with a sucking sound. As if searching for something lost at sea, we watched the sun sink below the horizon. The afterglow was a soft lavender that seemed more like daybreak than twilight. I put my arm around her, and she leaned against me. In the pass, tarpon were rolling. Their great silver bodies arched, gleaming in the dying light.

# THE SOOTHSAYER

IT IS AFTERNOON, a hazy Tuscany afternoon. I've hired a man to drive me to Fiesole, a village on a small mountain overlooking Florence. I am curious to see Fiesole because I have read in a guidebook that it once was the soothsaying center of the Roman Empire.

This is the summer of my son Jack's graduation from high school. When my daughter graduated, I took her to England because England is a country of great women: Mary Queen of Scots, Queen Elizabeth, Virginia Woolf, Cicely Saunders. I thought Italy, with its great men—Leonardo, Dante, Michelangelo—was the place a mother should take her son. I had made plans to bring Jack with me, but he allowed his father, my ex-husband, to steal him away on a salmon fishing expedition to Alaska. He'll come home barely in time for me to get his shirts back from the laundry, pick out a comforter and rug for his dorm room, and pack him off to Northwestern to start his freshman year. That he's leaving home seems impossible. When I think of him, it's as a small boy. Red wagon, blue bike, yellow bus. Things seemed like they would roll on forever, and now they're years ago.

So here I am alone, wandering Fiesole's labyrinth of narrow streets, searching for some remnant of the soothsayers, hoping, I suppose, to find some modern prophet who can look into my future and assure me I won't be trampled by the Four Horsemen of the Empty Stable: Self-pity, Boredom, Uselessness, Loneliness. Before Jack and his sister were born, I was an Obstetrician and Gynecologist building my practice. Surgery was my delight. I loved the challenge of a radical hysterectomy or the joy of delivering a newborn by Caesarean section. But I sacrificed my career for motherhood and housewifery. I've considered returning to medicine, maybe as an outpatient gynecologist or working for Planned Parenthood, but after all these years, my skills and knowledge have left me. I could never be a decent doctor again. When I look into the future, I see myself wearing wrinkled cotton and linen and heavy silver jewelry, traveling alone to the Islands. With a drink in my hand, I walk the shores, turning over shells.

Now I explore an ancient Franciscan church with a sanctuary of gray stone walls, heavy wooden beams and dusty light. I wander through the arches of a Romanesque cloister into a cemetery where a photo of the deceased adorns each headstone. The faces of the departed make death seem intimate and give me a disquieted feeling about this place. I realize it's the simple truth: every relationship is doomed to end.

Soon I'm hot and my feet are swelling, so I stop at the Aurora Hotel to slip off my shoes and enjoy a quiet lunch. I worry about the edema in my legs. Is my heart beginning to fail? What next? Digitalis and diuretics? A pacemaker? The trattoria is on a lovely terrace surrounded by wisteria-draped walls and shaded by a canopy of trees. Vases of blue cornflowers decorate tables covered with white linen cloths. The restaurant is almost deserted except for a young woman and an old waiter in a white, double-breasted dinner jacket and a black bow tie. The woman sits alone and smokes a cigarette. Tanned and pretty, she's the very picture of girls I saw on the Lido beach with the tops of their bikinis lying in the sand. And there I was, white and flabby in a flower-print swimming suit with its matronly little skirt. Oh, to be thin and topless and tan.

I watch her pick the cornflower from the vase on her table and twirl it between her fingers, then stick it in her hair. The blue flower makes her look striking and festive. You can be sure if Jack were here, he would notice her, the fullness of her breasts, the shadowed hollows of her neck. The old waiter seats me by a fountain that bubbles musically near a statue of a headless Roman soldier. With a shaky hand, he fills a long-stemmed goblet with aqua minerale.

"Buon giorno," he says.

"Cheers," I say tiredly.

Thirsty, I drain the glass, and he fills it again. He hands me the menu then wearily rolls the dessert cart to the girl's table. It seems to require all of his strength. Frail and shaky, his lips are dusky, and he's short of breath, a "blue blower" we would say in medical school. I wonder if he has an occult malignancy. Parkinson's disease? Emphysema? Congestive heart failure? I get up and stand behind my chair, fill my lungs with crystal air, try to breathe in fresh spirit. Below are green islands of olive groves. Like ships' masts, slender umbrella pines sprout from the sea of Florence's red-tile roofs. There is such beauty that ambition and longing or even love shouldn't enter into this. To see it, I suppose I should feel exhilarated, privileged like a Medici. Instead, I feel lost in a landscape of loneliness.

I lean forward and place my hands on the back of the chair as if it were Jack's shoulders. His shoulders are wide and powerful, the shoulders of a swimmer. Jack was conference champion in the fifty-meter breaststroke and the individual medley. It seems like I've spent every weekend of my life lugging him off to swim in some steamy natatorium. I nearly tear up thinking of cleaning out his room when I get home. What am I going to do with his old trophies and ribbons, the glittery cardboard crown that says "King of Hearts" or his Grateful Dead posters? What will become of weekends? I remember when he shaved off his wavy red hair so he could slip through the water faster in the state meet. He looked ghastly, like a chicken embryo. Now he's let it grow long so that it crawls over his collar. I'm always after him to keep it trimmed, always trying to get him to stop wearing those ridiculous John Lennon glasses. Lord, his vision is perfect.

I remember my unhappiness, even anger, the day I realized I was pregnant with Jack. How could I practice medicine and raise two children with a husband who was always off somewhere with his cronies, golfing and pubbing and chasing the lassies? Jack was a failure of self-control in a moment of stupid desire. I hoped for a miscarriage. I called Mother and cried, expecting pity, but she said, "This will be the easy one. The child who will bring you the most pleasure." And she was right. Jack has always worked so hard to please me. Maybe I'm being punished now for not wanting him.

Over the top of my menu, I watch the Italian girl. She is dressed in a pink sleeveless blouse and toreador pants that show the lines of her panties. I could teach her a thing or two about fashion. Sultry. Alone. Available. I know my son would turn his chair to watch her. She's the sort of woman his father always noticed, and Jack, I am sorry to say, is acquiring his father's appetite for women.

The waiter, with his shock of white hair and bushy mustache, moves slowly toward my table. He totters, leaning forward as if he were bucking a wind.

"Do you like the view, Signora?" he asks.

"Of course," I say. "It takes your breath."

"And what have you decided?" His English is accented but easy to understand.

"The scampi Savine?" I ask. "How's the scampi?"

"It's very good, Signora. Served with fettucini. Everything served here is good."

"I'll have the scampi," I say, "and the carciofi as well."

"Excellent." He smiles at me. "And a nice white wine? Pitigliano perhaps."

"Pitigliano would be fine," I say, and I imagine Jack across the table in baggy khakis, a Hard Rock T-shirt, boat moccasins with no socks, a quizzical smile. I see him sprawled casually in his chair; he seems preoccupied, almost a stranger. I would ask, "How about you, Jack? What sounds good?"

"Spaghetti with clams," he would say.

"You can get that at home at the Spaghetti Factory. If you want pasta, why don't you try the cannelloni and fagotto. It's pasta wrapped around spinach. I'm sure it's delicious."

I can see my son roll his eyes and close his menu. "Think I'll stick with spaghetti and clams. That is, if it's all right with you, Mother."

"Then will that be all?" the waiter asks. "Scampi Savine, carciofi, and a glass of Pitigliano."

"Bring a bottle," I say.

He goes to the kitchen to place the order. When he returns, he serves me a white china bowl filled with a rich dark brown stew.

"Cibreo," he says. "It's a famous local dish of chicken innards and coxcombs. Compliments of the house."

I take a bite, then another. It tastes fabulous. It touches a chord that makes me think I must have been Tuscan in a previous life.

"Do you like Cibreo?" he asks.

"It's wonderful."

"It was my mother's recipe," he says.

While I eat the Cibreo, he hovers around my table, filling the wine glass, whisking away breadcrumbs with a knife blade, humming fragments of an opera. It's obvious that he has a marvelous voice. *"La Bohème?"* I ask.

He smiles and shakes his head. *"Madame Butterfly,"* he says. Then he warbles a passage of "The Star Spangled Banner." I remember that Puccini had worked the National Anthem into one of Pinkerton's numbers in "Butterfly." I wonder, is he singing *Madame Butterfly* because he realizes I'm lonely like Madame?

"At least I got Puccini right," I say.

"Yes, Puccini."

Jack is in love with music. He has a fine baritone voice. In my mind, I can hear him singing, and it brings a stir of emptiness. Below, I can see Giotto's bell tower and the dome of the Pitti Palace across the Arno, but I can't find the church of Santa Croce. "Signor, can you point out Santa Croce?"

"There," the waiter says. "It's over there." He moves close to me and points. I can smell his body odor, a sour-sweat smell that Italian waiters often have. I suppose it has something to do with garlic as well as not bathing. "It's the church with a white marble facade and green trim."

"Oh, yes, I see it. That's where I wanted to take Jack," I say. "I wanted him to see the tombs of Galileo, Machiavelli, and Michelangelo." I'm talking more to myself than to the waiter. "It's hard to imagine all those immortals buried under one roof. Just to be in their presence, something would have to rub off on a young man. That's why he ought to be here. To be in touch with genius and creativity."

The old man looks puzzled. I'm not surprised. It's not something a waiter would understand.

"Jack's your son?"

"Yes." I nod, staring at the church through dusty sunlight.

"Where is he?"

"Gone." I swallow to steady my voice. "He's left home."

"You have other children?"

"A daughter, but she's not at home either."

"Your food should be ready," he says. His voice is gentle, and our eyes meet in a moment of understanding. "I'll bring your scampi." His accent is thick, and I feel like I'm watching us in a Fellini movie. "Here, enjoy more wine. Do you like the Pitigliano?"

I nod. He fills my glass, dribbling wine on the tablecloth. Then he disappears into the kitchen.

I rummage through my purse and find a small Casio tape recorder. I carry it with me to listen to "Getting Along in Italian" tapes and to dictate notes to myself. I insert a recording of Jack soloing with the high school glee club in a medley of Gershwin songs. I've listened to it so many times, the tape is beginning to sound worn. I'll need to make a copy before it breaks.

The waiter returns with a tray balanced on his trembling, gnarly hand. Dishes rattle. In front of me, he places a white, gold-rimmed china plate with six shrimp on a bed of pasta surrounded by a rosette of artichoke leaves. A buttery odor rises in steam, but suddenly I have no appetite. It seems like eating is a consolation.

"*Buon appetito*," he says.

I can't bear solitude at mealtime. At home, if Jack is gone, I'll switch on the television and watch *General Hospital, This Old House,* or *Aerobics with Jake*—anything with people and voices to make it seem like someone is with me. I clamp on the earphones and start the recording. I'm aware of the Italian girl staring at me. I stare back and make her look away. She dabs her mouth with a napkin, then applies a pink lipstick that matches her blouse. I know it isn't right, but I can't help resenting her youth and beauty. I dip an artichoke leaf in drawn butter and suck the pulp while Jack sings "Begin the Beguine." His voice resonates with warmth and fine pitch, but it wavers just a bit with lack of confidence. In that way he is like me. When I was a resident at Woman's Hospital, I was petrified presenting patients at grand rounds. I've tried to coach Jack to relax, but he can't get over sounding nervous. I close my eyes and savor the song. With his voice capturing my mind, I sense that Jack's presence is real, and he, the ancient waiter, the young woman, and I become actors in a play on the shady terrace-stage. I rewind the tape and dip the last petal of the artichoke. The butter has turned cold and gelatinous. The old waiter rattles a dessert cart with wedges of cakes, raspberries, and meringue across the stone floor to my table. He refills my wine glass.

"Music?" he asks, pointing at the tape player.

"Yes, it's my son."

"He's a musician?"

"Perhaps." I pause for a second. "Well, yes. He's a singer. Would you like to listen?"

"I don't want to intrude."

"No. Here, please. Listen."

I trade him the tape recorder for a thin tart of apples and pears.

"Torta di mele," he says, pouring cream over the dish and dusting it with powdered sugar.

"Your mother's recipe?" I ask.

"No. This recipe is my barber's."

He fumbles with the tape recorder. I show him how the machine works. He takes it to a stool by a china cabinet and slips on the earphones. Anxiety accumulates in my chest, a mother wanting her child to do well. Soon his eyes are closed and his head is tipped, his chin resting on his chest. His fluffy white hair falls forward so that it looks as if his face is in a cloud. He hums softly and taps his fingers with the music.

While I eat the torta, Jack's face comes into focus.

It's not downy like a boy's, but a young man's face with a whisker shadow on a prominent jaw. I pose the question that I wanted to bring Jack to Italy to ask. I say, "Jack what plans do you have for yourself? What have you decided to study? You're starting college. Don't you think it is time you were thinking about it?"

I see Jack gaze at his wine glass, move his hands over it, pretending it's a crystal ball, making a joke out of his answer. "I'll be a singer," he says. "I'll write music and sing like Billy Joel."

"And live with Christie Brinkley in the Caribbean," I say and chuckle. "That sounds fun. I'll visit you in the Islands, but I refuse to go to Las Vegas to see you perform."

Then under the spell of Santa Croce, the tone of my inner voice turns serious. "But I hoped you would want to go to medical school, to become a doctor like your grandfather and your mother. You used to talk about it all the time."

Jack pushes back his plate and folds his napkin. "I've changed my mind," he says. "I'm squeamish. I can't get into the sight of blood. I'm not really cut out for medicine."

"Nonsense," I say. "Don't be silly. You're excellent in science. So good with people. You'll be a wonderful doctor." I lean forward. Our gazes touch. The perfume of flowering shrubs drifts on a breeze. "Just think. After college you'll go to Johns Hopkins. Maybe you'll decide to become a surgeon. I loved the operating room and so will you." Then I say, "Just think. Maybe we could practice together someday."

Jack doesn't answer. He plays with his fork and shakes his head. My head is spinning; I pour more wine into my glass.

"Chill off." That's what he says. "Just chill off, Mom. Give me a break."

He says it with cruel finality, as though it is the end of everything between us. It's the way his father said things. Suddenly I'm on the verge of tears. Wine does this to me.

The woman I've been observing stands up, a slender, olive-skinned siren. She places money on the table, and Jack eyes her. "Listen, Mom. Think I'll head back down to Florence. I'll grab a bus in front of the hotel. Right to the Duomo. I want to climb the bell tower and check out the Gates of Paradise."

"And what about me?" I glare at him. It's the wine talking. "What did you have in mind for your mother?"

The young woman turns and walks by my table, and for the first time I see her face at close range. I'm startled. She wears a heavy layer of rouge to hide the pockmarks on her cheeks. She has dark facial hair on her upper lip and sideburns suggestive of a hormonal imbalance, possibly an endocrine tumor. There are deep lines under her eyes. She looks careworn.

"Hi," she says, a sad American "hi."

I want to call her back, to invite her to sit down with me and drink a cup of coffee. I want to tell her that I too am alone. Maybe we could meet tomorrow for dinner somewhere in the city, but she disappears through the stone archway of the hotel.

I empty the last of the Pitigliano into my glass and drink it. From my purse, I take a mirror to check my makeup. Mascara streaks my cheeks, and my lipstick is smeared. I realize I'm drunk. I think of standing up and in slow motion, toppling off the terrace, tumbling headlong down the mountain among rocks and yucca plants, ripping my hose, abrading my body. I shouldn't drink wine. With a Kleenex, I dab my cheeks, then touch up my lipstick, try to pull myself together. The air has cooled, and I gather a sweater around my shoulders, then call for the check. The old waiter brings it with the cassette player on a silver tray.

"Bravo," he says patting his hands together. "Thank you for sharing."

"You liked it?"

"Oh, yes. I love George Gershwin."

I count out lire which he tucks in to a worn leather wallet.

"Grazie," he says softly. I answer with a tired prego.

He turns and starts to shuffle across the terrace.

"Signor," I call to him. I want him to come back so he can tell me what he thinks of Jack's voice. "Maybe you can tell me. I'm curious about the soothsayers. Are there still soothsayers in Fiesole?"

The old man chuckles. I have the feeling that his watery gray eyes can look inside me as if I were transparent.

"Soothsayers," he says. "No. Not since Roman times."

I notice how pallid and frail he looks, how he seems almost translucent. I imagine his face, like a death mask, in one of the photographs on the gravestones.

"Sit down," I say. "You need to rest."

I pull out a chair for him, and stiffly, the old waiter sits down, his face grimacing as his arthritic knee joints crack.

"It's good to get off my feet," he says. "My bones are tired." He points at the cassette. "Your boy has a fine voice. He just need to let it come from here." He billows out his chest and pretends to raise his diaphragm with his hands. "Vigaro, vigaro, vigaro."

The volume of his voice is startling, and I laugh.

"I've told him the same thing without the vigaros. You have a magnificent voice. You've sung professionally?"

"After the war, I was with a small opera company in London. We performed all over Europe."

"Ah. I was wondering where you learned your English."

"Just a minute," he says and he stands up. "I'll be right back."

"I'm keeping you from your work," I say. "I must go."

"No. Don't leave. We need cappuccino. I'll bring us some."

He goes to the kitchen and returns with two small cups on saucers. The drink is hot and frothy with a rich coffee smell. I stir in sugar with a spoon.

"There's nothing like our cappuccino," he says. "Try some." He settles into the chair across from me. "You wear unhappiness like a Madame Butterfly. I think you miss the boy a great deal."

"Yes." I stare into the distance beyond the green hills and red roofs of the city. "I can't believe he's leaving. I feel empty, frightened of the future."

"I know how hard it must be," he says. "I was thinking of the boy. What it must be like for him. I remember how I felt leaving for England when I was young. Remember what leaving home was like?"

Among the empty tables, the sunlight slants through the leaves. The old man's face is a mask of shadows. Light and shadows. My mind flickers. I think for a moment, then I say, "It was like stepping out of dim light into sunshine and finally you're casting your own shadow."

"Yes," the old waiter says. "That's a nice way to put it." The old world rings in his accent. "Freedom, independence, growing up. I remember there was a feeling of relief, but more than anything, I think it was frightening."

"Frightening," I say. "And lonely." I sip the cappuccino, savor the bittersweet taste. "You know, I am trained as a doctor, but since my son was born, I've been mainly a mother. Now that being a mother is over, I don't know what I'm going to do with myself."

"I'm nothing like a doctor," he says. "I'm just a waiter." He pauses a moment and sips his cappuccino.

Feeling like we're old friends, I lean forward and listen.

"I guess that's all I'll ever be, someone who serves food and drink."

"There's not that much difference between a waiter and a physician," I say. "Both take care of people. Listen to what they want. Try to make them feel good."

"Yes," he says, smiling. "I like it when young people come into the restaurant. Especially for a party. Everyone is laughing. Sometimes there will be accordion music and dancing, then they'll ask me to sing. When I look into my future, that's all I see. People coming in to be fed, then leaving. A little music. That's what you need to do. Get back to taking care of people."

"I don't know. It's been a long time. Things have changed."

"You could do it."

"I don't know. The idea frightens me."

"Sure it does. It's like leaving home again."

We sit there drinking cappuccino and talking until the sky has turned lavender and the sun is low and orange. I realize the shadows of the trees are reaching all the way across the terrace. Finally my driver comes, and wearily, the old waiter gets to his feet.

"It's time to get to work." He smiles at me and takes my hand. His voice seems to come from a distance. "We just have to get used to it," he says.

"Used to what?"

"To being alone. Goodbye now."

AT DUSK, I stroll alone on the Ponte Vecchio, looking in shop windows at dazzling gold jewelry and dark leather. I buy my daughter earrings and Jack a travel bag. From the bridge, I look down at the Arno, its water as brown as wrinkled khaki. The brown water, flowing toward the dark hills beyond the city, dims and dissolves into the mist. I listen to the vesper bells toll and watch a sculler row a sliver of a boat under the bridge. Rhythmically, he dips his oars, pulls and strains, his legs pumping like pistons.

Before I head back to the hotel, I pay a sidewalk artist to sketch my portrait in charcoal. In fading light, I look at the picture and see what the artist has seen: a slim woman with a few wrinkles and pale, melancholy eyes. I smile, thinking I should have a cornflower in my hair.

# IF THE TASTE IS BITTER

ON THE BEACH in front of my house, I waded bare-footed in the shallows, watching two big snook feeding on a school of silver sardines. The early sun was bright and sparkled on motionless turquoise water. The scent of baked salt was in the air, and the chirping of shore birds came from every direction. I loved being there alone. It was these cool quiet mornings on the beach and the orange and lavender sunsets over the Gulf of Mexico that enticed me to buy the property twenty-five years ago, vowing to never again live without a view of water.

The snook darted off to some other prey. I turned to look at my seaside haven, a contemporary wooden structure with a wall of windows that offered a panoramic view of the Gulf of Mexico. Just this morning, in accordance with my divorce settlement, I had signed the papers to sell the house. Now my heart dropped in my chest seeing what had once been my home perched precariously on stilt-like concrete pilings. I felt as one must feel watching his home vanish in a hurricane.

The divorce from my wife, Ceci, had been bitter, filled with anger and blame. The sale of the house, forced on me by her and her attorney, was her final act of revenge. I walked from the beach through ever-shifting dunes where sea oats clung by their roots. Burning sand caked my wet feet. The air, heavy and hard to breathe, pressed down on me. It seemed to pin me to the ground.

"Goddamn you, Ceci," I thought.

I hosed off the sand from my ankles and toes and slipped into a pair of docksiders. In the side yard, I spotted Vinh, a Vietnamese refugee I had hired a couple of years ago as a part-time gardener and handyman. With a broom, he swept up the leaves from under a banyan tree. The roots hung from its limbs like tangled hair. Vinh was taller than the Vietnamese I knew in 1967 when I was a Green Beret corpsman in the Mekong Delta. His skin was the color of cashews. He wore the coarse cotton shirt and tire-tread sandals of a peasant. A length of clothesline held up his baggy dark pants. I couldn't look at him without remembering my year in his country during the war. Cold-sweat fear in a chopper waiting to be dropped into the jungle. Body bags and the stink of napalm. The war marked the end of any innocence that remained of my youth. It seemed that ever since, my life had been spent in a combat zone of one sort or another. I considered myself peaceloving and non-confrontational; I never understood why I ever let myself go to war. And then kept doing so.

At Vinh's feet today an old portable cassette player broadcast a scratchy rendition of Debussy's *La mer*. Vinh believed music made the plants happy and enhanced their growth. His melodious fertilizer worked. The blossoms of the gardenias and bougainvillea he tended were always fresh and fragrant, the ferns and calla lilies exceptionally green. As I walked through the gardens, the hair on the back of my neck bristled. Not only was I being evicted from my dream house, I was being expelled from Eden.

For a moment, I watched Vinh work. His broom swung slowly in rhythm with the waves that lapped the shore. A mysterious smile shone on his face as if he knew something I didn't know. I am a retired orthopedic surgeon. In the operating room, reconstructing a knee or pinning a hip, I was fast and efficient, decisive, impatient when I needed to be. Vinh's pace frustrated me. But even though he was slow and contrary, I liked him. Opposites do attract. I had been an accomplice in the atrocities committed against his people during the war. No doubt, there something about supporting a refugee from Nam that eased my conscience. I regretted having to tell him that his days in the garden here were finished.

As I approached the tree where he worked, he nodded and kept on swinging the broom evenly, a human metronome.

"There's a leaf blower in the garage that might work better," I said.

"Broom is fine," he said.

"Leaf blower is faster," I said. "I'm paying you by the hour."

I meant it as a joke.

"Broom fast enough. Do better job. No noise."

He stopped sweeping and looked up at me with a broad smile. A gold tooth gleamed.

"What's the matter, Bacsi?" Vinh said. "You look upset today."

"You're damn straight I'm upset," I said. "I've been forced to sell this beautiful house. I just accepted a low-ball offer."

"Why you sell, if you like house?"

"The divorce, old friend. I can't afford it since the pie got cut in two. Taxes. Hurricane insurance. The carrying costs of owning the place are just too much for me to handle."

"Don't be upset, Bacsi," Vinh said. "These things happen."

"Easy to say," I said.

Vinh grew up in a thatched roof hut and now lived in a rented trailer off-island. What would he know about my feelings or the pride of ownership of prime ocean-front property?

"Not only did I have to sell the house," I said, "my ex knew the bind I was in. She wouldn't agree to the sale unless I gave her a hundred grand more than I got." For a moment, I pictured men that looked like Vinh coming toward me out of the smoke and mist. Why was I telling him this? "It was pure extortion. Grand larceny. She might as a well have put a gun to my head."

I watched Vinh's face for a reaction. His expression was noncommittal.

"I loved this goddamn house," I said, shaking my head in disbelief. It seemed impossible that the property was no longer mine. "I would have left it to my daughter, Sally. It was my dream."

"Dreams," he scoffed. "All fantasy and doubt. Not worth clinging to, Bacsi."

"Come on. Without dreams you might as well be dead." For an instant, I panicked, realizing I was dreamless. "You believe in the American dream? That's why you came here for God's sake?"

"American dream is looking for something that isn't there. I came here to find a job. That's all."

Then why don't you go back to the goddamn rice paddies, I wanted to say.

What I did say was: "Listen, Vinh, the closing is in a month. I'm sorry but you're going to be out of a job. The people who bought the house are going to tear out all of these plantings and put in a swimming pool and pool house. They won't need a gardener. At least for a while."

There. That shook his complacency. And satisfied me in the bargain.

"Maybe they need lifeguard," Vinh said. "Or maybe cabana boy." He thought a moment. "Why the hell they want swimming pool?" He pointed toward the Gulf of Mexico where sunlight wove a silver tapestry on the waves of the blue-green water. "They have whole ocean to swim in."

"Who knows," I said. "They're Wall Streeters with more money than sense. Maybe they're afraid of sharks."

"Ah," Vinh said, flashing his gold-toothed smile again. "I see. Pirañas afraid of sharks. Don't worry about my job. I find something else to do."

"Like what?"

"My wife has nail salon. Maybe I become specialist like you. A cuticle specialist."

A dragonfly landed on the fly of my khaki shorts and clung to the cloth. I looked down at it and for the first time today, smiled.

"She likes you," Vinh said. "I think it's an omen. Your luck with women will change. Things get better for you."

"Yeah, right," I said as the blue insect flew away on transparent wings. "Fat chance."

TWO WEEKS after the contract for the sale of the house had been signed, I walked from room to room with a yellow notepad, a ballpoint pen, and digital camera. It was time for Ceci and me to divide up the furnishings as mandated by the court. I made a meticulous inventory of the contents of my "dream" and took a picture of each relic of our thirty-five years of marriage. If there was an equation between happiness and processions, our life together should have been euphoric. Everywhere I looked there was something attractive and tasteful to see —expensive furniture we had picked out on a trip with an interior decorator to the furniture mart in Chicago, family heirlooms, art by artists we had known. On the wall of the entryway was a terra-cotta sculpture of a man and woman joined by an arch formed by two trees that grew from their heads like flames from a fire.

When the inventory was complete, I sat on a barstool at the granite-topped kitchen counter. For a moment, I looked out the window at two gulls on the beach squabbling over the carcass of a mackerel. They flew at each other pecking and scolding, playing tug-of-war with the dead fish in their beaks. In front of me was my Macintosh laptop computer and the yellow notepad. Since it was impossible for Ceci to talk with me without getting angry, I had decided it was best to carry out the division of the furnishings by e-mail. Although I was eager to break marital bonds and get on with my life, the finality of the process gave me pause. Everything in the house had been purchased with money earned by me bending over an operating table for hours or setting a fracture in the middle of night. But somehow, I knew Ceci would come out of this with more than I would. She always managed to have her way. I took a deep breath, booted up my iBook, and opened "mail."

I selected "new" and wrote: "Ceci, we both have plenty of stuff. I think we should let Sally take what she wants, then we can split the rest by alternate choices."

I hit "send," pleased with my largesse. I am a generous man. Like invisible birds, my words whooshed away into cyberspace.

Ceci responded immediately.

"If you want to give Sally things from your list that's up to you. I'm planning to use mine to furnish Dan's and my new condo in Naples."

I felt the blood leave my face. Ceci had recently remarried a man with a 64-foot Sunchaser yacht and his own quail-hunting preserve. He was nearly eighty. Seventeen years older than she was. Before he retired,

Dan ran his family's savings and loan banks. If they needed things, he could buy them.

"I'll go first," she concluded. "I want the shell stone table."

Oh right, I thought. Of course, you'll go first. It was so Ceci. I clicked on "reply" and typed, "I'm not sure why you should go first. Usually a coin is flipped and the person who gets the second choice is allowed the second and third choices. Then the alternate choice proceeds with the number one chooser getting the fourth choice and so on. If you agree to my having the next two choices then you can have the first choice. Otherwise we'll flip a coin or something."

I centered the arrow over "send" and punched the mouse hard. Within seconds the e-mail bell on my MAC dinged.

"What's the deal?" she fired back. "When we set this up, you said I could go first. I went. Is there anything that says if I choose first you get the next two choices? First time I've heard that one. Little hard to flip a coin when we're NOT IN THE SAME AREA. Obviously, you wanted that table, too. We don't always get what we want, do we?"

I laughed when I read the part about it being hard to flip a coin when you weren't in the same area. I wondered if she was being serious or just ridiculous. She did have a sense of humor, usually at my expense or

Sally's. So maybe she was just being a wise guy? I knew she hated me. Something about her hatred made me feel good.

I thought for a moment. Although it was the most expensive piece of furniture in the house, I really didn't want the shell stone table. It weighed a ton and would be an expensive pain in the ass to move and there was no room for it in the apartment I was renting. So if I let her have it, in effect, I would be getting my first choice.

I typed, "Oh, Princess. Go first. It's just stuff." I thought a moment. Too strong. Too confrontational. Rise above the fray. I changed "Princess" to "Ceci:" "Oh, Ceci, go first. It's just stuff. The shell stone table is yours. I'll take the blue and rust Indian rug from Santa Fe. Let's do ten picks today and then take a break, and do some more tomorrow."

I knew she loved the rug and would want it. I sent the message boldly with a sense of triumph.

While I waited, I looked at the rug spread under a teak coffee table with its beautiful pattern of hexagons and parallelograms in shades of blue, rust, and beige. I remembered the summer vacation in New Mexico when we bought the Navaho carpet. We stayed at Rancho Encantada, where celebrities like Henry Fonda, Fran Tarkington, and Princess Anne had stayed. The wrangler taught Sally how to ride a horse. Ceci and I took a set off the tennis pro, a fellow Vietnam veteran, and his girlfriend. We went to the open-air opera and saw a wonderful performance of *Der Rosenkavalier*. I recalled how bright the stars over the desert were that night. For an instant my chest felt empty.

Ceci's response flashed onto the computer screen: "Fine! Take the rug. I'll take the Travertine marble coffee table in the living room."

Another heavy monstrosity I didn't want. A smile came to my lips.

For a while, we went back and forth swapping choices: the teak coffee table for a walnut sideboard, a sofa for a king-sized bed and headboard, a signed Calder print for a Robert Indiana lithograph, a Cheret poster for Kuba cloth acquired on a camera safari in Kenya. When I took the steamer chest that had been my grandmother's, Ceci responded that she was glad I had taken it because it was from my grandmother, whom she knew I adored. Her uncharacteristic display of compassion rocked me back a bit. This was easier to do when she was contentious. But the interlude of kindness was brief. When I selected a wicker couch and matching chair, she returned to form and wrote: "I'm very upset by the way you chose both the chair and the couch at the same time. This is deteriorating into something unpleasant. If it continues that way, I'll stop and dust off old Marvin."

The threat of Ceci involving her divorce attorney, a pit bull of a man in an Armani suit and jewelry, reminded me of the mediation Ceci had walked out on. The court-appointed mediator, a young female lawyer who had tried unsuccessfully to bring us to compromise, said: "Doctor, she will torture you with the house." How right she had been. Why had I married someone so vindictive and selfish, someone obsessed with land and money? How could I have been so stupid?

"Okay then," I keyboarded. "If you want it that badly, you can have the damn chair. I'll keep the couch. For my next choice, I'll take the Brown Jordan porch furniture. You should take the Steuben glass apple. An apple a day keeps the doctor away."

While I waited for her answer, I looked out the window and watched Vinh trimming the sea grapes by the garage. He had tied a white handkerchief around his forehead as a sweatband so that he looked like a Viet Cong. He put down his hedge clippers and walked to an orange tree laden with ripe fruit that grew by the driveway. The sun was at his back, and the shadow of his thin body moved in front him at an angle. For a moment, I saw him through the cross hairs of a sniper's gunsight. Ever since the war, there were times when I felt like a claymore mine about to be detonated.

For what seemed like a long while, Vinh studied the oranges and then he picked one. He carried it to the banyan tree and sat cross-legged on the ground at its base as he did when he drank the chrysanthemum tea and cracked the pumpkin seeds he often brought to work. For a while, he stared at the orange in his hands, breathing and smiling, his lips moving in what must have been some sort of prayer. I kept glancing from him to the computer screen, looking for a reply from Ceci. Finally, Vinh pulled a folding knife from his pocket. He opened it and skillfully peeled the orange, handling the blade as if it were a scalpel and the fruit a spinal cord's tumor. When he was finished, he arranged the pieces of rind in a pattern in the sand beside him. He broke off a segment and chewed it slowly. Jesus, I thought, hurry up before it rots.

The computer bell dinged. I opened Ceci's latest hate mail.

"I'll take the four paintings by Vito Tori above the bed," she wrote.

"Goddamn it," I said aloud.

The brightly colored acrylics were magically realistic landscapes done by an Italian artist from whom we'd rented a villa in Umbria one summer not too long ago. During our stay, I had become a good friend of Vito's. We went to local soccer games, walked his German shepherd up the mountain in the morning, and drank Chianti together at a neighborhood trattoria in the afternoon. I was quite fond of him and his work. Ceci thought him loud and self-centered, and she didn't care for his paintings. I had been certain they wouldn't appear on her list. I knew she was taking them just to spite me. If I had suspected she was going to do that, I would have chosen them first.

Seething, I punched the "quit" command. The computer sighed and went to sleep.

I walked outside to where Vinh, still eating the orange, was now squatting on his heels. I always marveled at the way Vietnamese hunkered on their haunches over a pot of rice or a basket they were weaving. If I had tried to assume that position, I would have ruptured tendons and torn ligaments.

"How's it going, Bacsi?" he asked.

"I'm in a battle royal," I said. I looked at the circular pattern Vinh had created in the sand with the fragments of the orange rind, something a child might have done.

"What are you doing with the orange, playing Truyen-Truyen?" I said, remembering the game Vietnamese children played in the dirt with sticks and a round fruit.

"Making sort of a mandala, I guess." With the back of his hand, he brushed the fragments of orange peel away. "You say you in battle. How you in battle?"

"My ex and I are splitting up the furnishings of the house. It's war. It's like the Tet Offensive."

"Tet very bad. Many Vietnamese get killed. Dividing possessions not like Tet." He looked up at me with his head tilted in a quizzical way. "What you afraid of, Bacsi?"

"Why nothing. Why did you ask that?"

"You say you in war. Root of all wars is fear."

I thought for a moment.

"I don't buy that. Wars can be fought for the sake of justice. Defending what's right against an evil enemy."

"War itself is the enemy," Vinh said. "It can't be poverty you afraid of. You have plenty money. Must be something else."

From the driveway of the house next door, my neighbor's golden retriever appeared. The big dog trotted down the sand road to Vinh and began licking the orange juice from his fingers. Vinh scratched the dog's head.

"Yellow dog taste better than black dog," he said with an impish smile.

The golden must have understood what Vinh said because he barked at Vinh and fled.

"My ex-wife is one vindictive woman," I said. "Do you know why divorces cost so much, Vinh?"

"Don't know."

"Because they're worth it," I said.

Vinh smiled but didn't laugh.

"Why you think she that way, so vindictive?" he said.

"Who knows and who cares. If I did know, it wouldn't change her."

"Might change you, Bacsi." Vinh spit out a seed and wiped his lips. "Make you calm instead of mad."

I needed sympathy and confirmation, not a Sunday school lesson.

"She's greedy," I said. "The only thing she wouldn't do for money is work. She just married some rich old sugar daddy twice her age. What's that make her? What else is there to understand about her?"

Vinh shrugged his shoulders. He broke off a segment of the orange he had been eating and handed it to me.

"Here," he said. "Enjoy this."

I took a bite. The fruit was pithy, the pulp dry.

"Orange delicious," Vinh said. "Don't you agree?"

I was too angry at Ceci to taste anything but the acid that boiled up in my esophagus.

"It's okay," I said. "A little sour."

He held up the last remaining segment of the orange.

"If the taste is bitter," he said, "don't blame the orange."

BACK IN THE KITCHEN, I booted the computer. Nervously, I opened the e-mail from Ceci that awaited me. What did she want from me now? The Zuni pottery bowl with my testicles in it.

"I just asked for the Tori quadripictic and haven't

heard back. What's the deal? I thought you wanted to wrap this up. What's your next choice?"

I wrote back: "Quadripictic? I'm not familiar with that term, but I suppose it means four pictures." Like a wily boxer, I didn't want her to know she had hurt me with her blow. "I wanted to donate them to MOMA for a big tax write-off, but they're yours in all their glory. I'll take the dining room table and chairs and give them to Sally. She needs them more than we do."

I leaned back against the wall and waited, picturing Ceci the last time I saw her. It was nearly a year ago and soon after her return from rehabilitation at Betty Ford. We met accidentally and awkwardly on Sally's front porch: Ceci was leaving; I was arriving. I was startled by the metamorphosis my wife had undergone. It was as if she were a character in a Kafka story. Ceci's body had taken on a new slimmer shape. The pouches under her eyes and her crow's feet were gone. The loose skin of her neck appeared to have been surgically tightened, the spider veins on her calves lasered. She was dressed in a punk-rock-style leather miniskirt that showed off her long but aging legs, and a tight turtleneck that displayed her ample breasts. Her hair was shoulder length and straight as a sorority girl's. It struck me as sad, Ceci trying to be someone she wasn't. Or perhaps I was seeing who she really was.

"You look good," I said, although I didn't think she did.

"So do you," Ceci answered in a quavering voice. I sensed there was a longing bottled up in her that she wanted to let out, but she turned and hurried away to her car.

The computer bell dinged. I placed a finger on the mouse and clicked it.

"Hello. Are you there? You have chosen the dining room table and chairs. You assumed they go together. So the big TV and Bose sound system would go together, too. If the speakers can be moved, that would be my next choice."

The speakers were built into a cabinet that would have to be totally dismantled.

"Choices aren't conditional," I responded. "As Mother used to say, 'a card laid is a card played.' You asked for them, so you've got them." I glanced out the gulf-side windows at what had become a turbulent and hostile ocean. The sun was strange and muted by the dense humidity in the atmosphere. "It's a beautiful day down here and snook are biting. I'm calling it a day and going fishing."

In a few seconds, the e-mail bell on the Mac dinged. I started to reach for the mouse, but I thought better of it and put the computer to sleep. For a while, I worked on the inventory list, initialing the items that had been chosen. In the order of desirability, I numbered the possessions that remained. The Lenox Christmas china I gave a high ranking because I liked it, the sterling silver candelabra because I knew it would be valuable when sold at a consignment shop. As I pondered the value of tablecloths and bed linens, a feeling of weariness came over me. The selection process revolted me. How had my life come to this? I sat chewing on the tortoise shell earpiece of my glasses while staring off into space, yearning for something deeper and truer. Just who are you, doctor? I wondered. What are you afraid of?

Vinh was right, I had all the money I needed. Could it be that I was afraid of letting a woman get the better of me? And what was Ceci's fear that made her angry and drove her to drink? The bickering with her had exhausted me. I moved to the living room and settled onto the couch. I closed my eyes, hoping to sleep. But in a few seconds a knock sounded on the door. I dragged myself to the entry where Vinh stood. Sweat streamed down his face. His shirt was damp and clung to him. I invited him in and offered him a cold beer. He declined and asked for water. With a tall, beaded glass in his hand, he sat at the bar stool beside me and drank slowly.

"What do I owe you?" I asked.

"Don't worry. We can settle up later. How's battle going?"

"Back and forth," I said. "There's no clear winner at this point."

"Wars never have clear winner. Both sides lose."

He downed what remained of his water and set the glass on the counter.

"I've been thinking of your situation, Bacsi. It remind me of story my father tell me when I teenage boy. We on boat in South China Sea leaving Vietnam when war was lost. Everything was lost for us. House. Family. Animals. Even my mother not with us. She stay behind with my sister, Phuong, to take care of her old mother."

As Vinh talked, he drew a circle with his finger in the wet ring the water glass had left on the counter. Then he wiped it away as he had done the orange peel pattern in the sand.

"Before the war, my father a farmer in Mekong Delta. It very beautiful there like here. He raise ducks and chickens. He sell their feathers and eggs, not their meat. But this story not about birds. It about cows."

"Good," I said, remembering the neighbor's dog licking Vinh's fingers. "I was afraid it was going to be about eating old Fido." I looked at my watch. "Go ahead. Get to the story. I've got some calls to make."

"One day long ago, an old monk dressed in a saffron robe sit on log under shady tree, talking with young monks. Old farmer came, walking slowly, looking unhappy and angry."

"Monks," farmer say. "Have you seen my cows?"

"No, man," say old monk. "No cows have come by here."

"My cows ran away," the farmer said. "The bugs eat my crops. I have no crops. No cows. I have nothing. I think I kill myself."

"Very sorry, sir," old monk say. "No cows here. Look somewhere else for your cows."

"Farmer leave with his head down very sad. When he out of sight old monk smile and say to young monks, 'You very lucky. You very happy. You have no cows to lose.'"

I thought for a moment. Then I raised my eyes from the floor and looked at Vinh. Vinh looked back at me. The gaze of his bright almond eyes seemed to penetrate through the pupils of my eyes into the depths of my brain. I nodded my head.

THE DAY the movers were to come empty the house, the wind shifted and there was a cooling sea breeze out of the west. The tide was low, the sand the color of polished ivory. When I took my last morning walk on the wide crescent beach, there were no tourists, only shells and me. The previous night a loggerhead turtle had dragged herself up onto the dunes and laid her eggs among the sea oats. Her flippers' tracks formed a vee in the sand. Vinh would call her trail from the water to the dune and back a symbol of the cyclical nature of life. My leaving the house and the new owner moving in were part of that infinite coming and going. I removed my shoes and continued down the beach. The scent of salt and seaweed filled the air. I waded knee-deep into the surf. For a long time, I stood, staring at tranquil, jade-green water, letting the sea soothe me.

IN THE EARLY AFTERNOON, Honeymoon Haulers, a fly-by-night moving company from Miami, came in an old eighteen-wheeler to collect Ceci's loot and the furniture I had given Sally. I thought "Divorce Distributors" would have been a more appropriate monicker. The driver of the truck, a bearded man in a turban, backed the trailer into the banyan tree and tore off a big limb that now blocked the driveway. I shook my head in disbelief and managed to laugh. Then I helped his crew drag the limb off the road.

When the moving truck pulled away, I surveyed what remained of the furnishings and household items. The Kuba cloth wallhanging seemed shoddy, the Japanese hibachi worthless. I decided to only keep the Indian rug from Santa Fe. I called Vinh and offered him everything else. He said his sister Phuong had emigrated from Vietnam and was moving into an apartment near his trailer park. She would be grateful for anything I might give her.

In a little while, Vinh and Phuong appeared in a blue pickup truck. Phuong was a beautiful woman, slim in toreador slacks, her long black hair luxuriant and streaked with gray. Her eyebrows were high and arched. She told me she had taught French in a school in Vung Tau, a city on the South China Sea, where I had taken an in-country R & R during the war. She was someone I would like to know better.

When we finished loading Phuong's things into the truck, Phuong and Vinh helped me clean the house. We worked until dusk. We vacuumed carpets, scrubbed out tubs and toilets, and carried out bags of trash. When Vinh wiped down the shelf of a closet in the den, he found a family photo album that I had missed.

He handed it to me and said, "War over, Bacsi."

"Yeah. Like you said, there was no winner."

"Takes time but wounds heal. It comes with understanding and forgiveness." Vinh patted me on the shoulder. "Here's the good thing, Bacsi. When you leave house tonight, you no have to lock door."

"Empty barn. No cows," I said.

After Vinh and Phuong were gone, I toured the house to make sure everything was ready for the realtor's final inspection. In the mirror over a bathroom sink, I read my age in the sagging, spotted parchment of my face. I thought how I and everything else had changed from the day I bought the house. Moving through vacant spaces over bare floors, I knew these were rooms I would never enter again. It was vital for me to remember them and the way the life of a small family had played out in them —the hurt, anger, and alienation, as well as the laughter and love. I swept up a dead cockroach that Vinh had missed when he vacuumed the carpets. The big bug's exoskeleton was crisp and dry. His antennae were long enough to pull in the Voice of America.

I thought again of Kafka's Gregor Samsa. It saddened me to think the insect was alone when he died. I set the air conditioner on eighty degrees, unplugged the water heater, and turned off the sprinkling system. In the light of a dying day, the immense silence of the walls announced that I was alone and that the voice of my past had been muted. I paused in front of a window to drink in the ocean view. Close the drapes, I thought. It's too beautiful. Then I said to myself, what a wonderful place to have lived. Why did you let it slip away? For a moment, my eyes glistened.

Satisfied that everything was in order, I went to the refrigerator and retrieved a bottle of champagne that I had chilled for the occasion. I spread the Indian rug in front of the window in the living room and sat on the floor crossed-legged, Vinh style. My muscles were fatigued. My arthritic shoulder and the tendinitis in my elbow ached from lifting and carrying. I felt as Sisyphus must have felt at the foot of the mountain, except I had champagne. I uncorked the bottle and poured a glass.

For a while, I sipped the sparkling wine and took my time paging through the photo album. There was a black-and-white picture of Ceci and me taken twenty-five years ago at a birthday party given for a friend in New York at the French consulate. Ceci wore a black sheath dress and I a tuxedo and black tie. We had been high-spirited that night, both a little tipsy. The photo showed us smiling and holding hands on the way up a wide marble stairway. Quite a couple. Many of the pictures were of Sally: an unspoiled girl of four in a swimsuit and sun bonnet, digging with a wooden spoon in the sand; there in the turn of a page, she was a long-legged teenager in a bikini sailing my Sunfish. On another page, she appeared as a college student with a beer and a boyfriend with big ears. It saddened me that the house wouldn't be hers someday. But there would be other places for her. You must believe that about your children. I closed the album and set it aside.

I stared at the Gulf, so calm and blue, breathing. Beyond the windows, palm fronds clacked in the evening breeze. Soon the sun dropped below the horizon. The sky glowed with streaks of orange and lavender. A flock of pipers rose from the shore and flew away. They darted and wove in the wind. Before long, darkness descended, deep and violet. I sat as still as Vinh might have sat, until the moon appeared between two clouds. It shone very pale at first, then turned bright. A lightness came over me. I felt as if I weighed no more than the moon's reflection on the water.

# THE DONOR

HAROLD ROBERT'S NINETEEN-YEAR-OLD SON, David, has no nose, eyelids, ears, or a right hand. They were burned off one night when he was on patrol in the Saydia neighborhood of Baghdad. A Sunni Jihadist hidden behind the wall of a mosque detonated a road-side bomb. The explosion hit the Humvee David was riding in, turning it into an inferno. The driver Lewis, a tall African-American corporal from Chicago, was killed instantly when the force of the blast blew a fragment of shrapnel through his Kevlar helmet and into his brain. Lewis was David's best Army buddy. Before every mission they shook hands in a complicated ghetto dance of fingers and told each other to "Fear no one Evil." When the medic pulled David out of the Humvee,

David's body armor was on fire. Using a fire extinguisher, the corpsman put out the flames.

AT DUSK the day the roadside bomb exploded, Harold was at the kitchen table in the townhouse apartment in Indianapolis where, since his separation from Tess, his wife of thirty years, he lives alone in the waning years of his general surgery practice. He had recently been cross-country skiing in Northern Michigan where he fell with the ski pole in his grasp, levering the thumb joint of his right hand and partially rupturing the ulnar collateral ligament of his thumb, the gamekeeper's injury. With his hand in an elastic-and-metal splint and unable to operate or play classical guitar, he was drinking Mount Gay rum and ginger ale to ease the pain while working a crossword puzzle left-handed. The codeine he had taken an hour ago was wearing off. The emptiness of the house and the dirty dishes in the sink reminded him that his marriage was over and his son was off to war.

While searching for a word for a succulent plant, his thoughts were on David. He pictured him in the sweltering Iraqi desert with his M16 at the ready. The ring of the telephone startled Harold. Certain that harm had come to David, he put down his pencil and picked up the receiver. In a solemn, faraway voice with a Virginian accent, Captain Hunter Keevil, David's company commander, told Harold that David had been hit by EFP and that he was in surgery receiving treatment for extensive burns and wounds. It was as if the blast from Bagjdad had traveled halfway around the world and hit Harold full force. He hung up the phone and slumped to the floor. While it turned dark, he sat, rocking back and forth and pressing his injured thumb against the floor to feel the pain.

During his surgical residency, Harold had worked in a burn unit, debriding charred flesh, grafting skin, and prescribing morphine. He considered burns the most painful and disfiguring of all injuries. It seemed impossible that his only child had been consumed by flames. Harold was not a follower of any religion. He didn't believe in prayers of entreaty, but that night he prayed for God to save his son from suffering, to take him quickly if that was what was needed to end his misery.

An hour later when the phone rang again, Harold rose from the floor to answer it. He heard Captain Keevil say David was out of surgery and alive, but that his right hand, the fingers of his left hand, and his right leg had been amputated. What David had been—and could have been—went up in smoke in the dark Iraqi sky. And he, Harold, was responsible for what had happened to his son.

~

TWO WEEKS LATER, Harold sits in a booth in The Alamo Coffee Shop in San Antonio near the Brooke Army Medical Center. The day before, David had been flown to Texas in a C-17 transport plane from Landstuhl Hospital in Germany where his burns were treated and his amputations completed. The diner is crowded and smells of hot bacon grease. On the walls are antique pistols and rifles and drawings of the Battle of the Alamo. Most of the customers seated at the counter are Army personnel dressed in desert fatigues the color of sand. Their boots are beige suede with lug soles. The uniforms remind Harold of his year as a battalion surgeon with the infantry in Vietnam and the fatigues and jungle boots he wore. The Army attire inflames his distaste for anything military.

Harold stares out the window at a cloudless morning sky that looks artificially blue and ominous. The sun blazes over a landscape of tall brick hospital buildings and scorched earth. He thinks of David before he went to war, an intelligent good-looking college boy, not handsome but clean-cut with kind blue eyes and a defiant chin. David was a loving, peaceful child, hardly someone whom Harold thought would be turned into a lethal weapon. Harold remembers how he loved to watch him sleep. When he bounced David on his knee and tickled him under his arms, David would laugh until his eyes watered, and he would beg Harold not to stop. Harold could tell how much the little boy loved him. Affection tore at his heart. He yearned to protect David from whatever adversity he would face.

Harold sips his coffee, remembering the day his own chaotic life imploded. It was Thanksgiving morning when a pimp named Carlos e-mailed Tess and David pictures of Harold in a room of a seedy Days Inn near the Indianapolis airport. High on rum and crack cocaine, Harold sat naked on the bed. Katya, a blond Russian prostitute with tongue-piercing jewelry, was on her knees between his legs. Carlos stole Harold's wallet and iPhone, then used the phone's camera to take Harold's picture. Harold had paid him five thousand dollars to not send the photographs. But when Carlos demanded five thousand more and Harold refused, the pictures were e mailed to the favorites listed in Harold's contacts. The coffee and the memory of what he had done make Harold's stomach churn. He feels nauseated. He wants to cry. His uninjured hand shakes, and the porcelain mug rattles on the saucer when he puts it down.

A teenage Hispanic waitress, dressed in jeans and a T-shirt that says "Remember the Alamo Coffee Shop," appears at the table with a pot in her hand. With a smile, she warms Harold's coffee.

"Gracias, Angela," Harold says, reading her blue name tag.

"De nada," she says. "Ready to order?"

Harold is waiting for Tess. The last time he was with her was a year ago when she told him she wanted him out of the house. No longer able to hide the dark truth of his double life, he had loaded his Land Rover with clothes, a few medical books, and his prized Friedrich guitar and left without an argument. Although they are living apart, they have agreed to visit David together and support him with a united front.

Harold looks at the silver Rolex on his wrist. Tess is already ten minutes late. In the months away from her, the very facts of Tess have begun to fade from his consciousness. Now he remembers how she always kept him waiting. He even misses her tardiness. Although he isn't hungry, Harold decides to eat something. From the menu, he chooses eggs over easy with sausage.

"Grits, hash browns, or biscuits and gravy?" Angela asks.

Harold no longer cares about cholesterol, exercise, and longevity.

"Oh," he says. "Biscuits and gravy, I guess."

"Gracias, amigo."

Angela leaves the table and hands the order slip to an old man with a handlebar mustache at the grill behind the counter. Harold watches the man crack eggs into a bowl. He wears a grease-splattered apron and a baseball cap with the insignia of the 2nd Infantry Division, the profile of a Native American Indian warrior in headdress superimposed on a star. Harold assumes the cook is a veteran of Korea. Every generation in America's history has had its war. Harold shakes his head, knowing that the shit of war will go on and on forever.

On the seat beside Harold is the morning edition of the *San Antonio Express-News*, stained with ketchup. He picks up the newspaper. George W. Bush's face stares at him from the front page. In the lapel of his navy-blue suit coat is an American flag stickpin. The President stands beside Specialist Rick Yardley, a victim of the Iraqi war who is at Brooke in the Defense and Veterans Brain Injury Center. There is a crater in the young soldier's shaved head where part of his skull had been surgically removed. His face is puffy and pale. He is smiling at the camera, but his eyes are dark and vacant. Harold reads that Yardley's brain was damaged when his Bradley fighting vehicle was blown up by an RPG. A shudder of revulsion passes through Harold.

The door to the diner opens and Tess steps through it. Harold watches her search the restaurant for him. His heart speeds. In the year since he last saw her, she has lost at least ten pounds. Her hair that was gray and short is frosted and long. Her leather skirt is brief, and like her hair style, he finds its length inappropriate for someone her age. There is something unfamiliar about her appearance that saddens Harold. Her gaze finds him, and he hails her with a wave.

Neither of them has yet filed for divorce, but Tess is dating Lou, an older insurance man she met at a Presbyterian singles group. Although their marriage was devoid of intimacy for years, Tess's new relationship causes Harold to feel something like loneliness but tinged with jealousy and guilt.

With her head down, Tess makes her way through the crowded restaurant. A wave of indecision sweeps over Harold. How should he greet her? With a hug? A kiss? A handshake? What should he say? Should he apologize or pretend nothing was wrong?

When she arrives at the table, Harold rises and embraces her. The press of her large breasts awakens his chest. He feels the moist heat of her skin through her silk blouse. The fragrance of her shampoo is familiar to him. He releases her, and she quickly retreats into the seat across from him. She looks at Harold as if he were a casual acquaintance met on the street.

"You look good," Harold says.

"I'm not good," she says. Her eyes appear tired and red like eyes that have been up all night crying. "Who could be good?" She points at the splint on his hand. "What happened?"

"A little boo-boo. A ski injury. My balance isn't what it once was."

"Too bad," Tess says. "I'll bet it kills you not to play your guitar."

"Yeah. I miss it."

"I miss hearing it," Tess says.

Harold nods. A long moment of awkward silence follows.

"Where are you staying?" Harold finally says.

"In an efficiency apartment in the Embassy Suites. It's near the hospital."

"How long do you plan to be in San Antonio?"

"As long as David is here," Tess says. "Where are you staying? In a Days Inn no doubt?"

Harold's face reddens at the reference to his infidelity.

"My Days Inn days are over. I'm in a mom-and-pop motel down the street."

Angela serves Harold a plate of eggs, link sausage, and a biscuit in a puddle of gray gravy. She pulls a pad and pencil from the waist of her jeans and smiles at Tess.

"Señorita?" she says.

"Just a cup of tea with lemon."

Harold hands Angela the soiled newspaper. The waitress nods at picture of the brain-damaged soldier.

"A real hero," she says.

"My son is at a patient at Brooke," Tess says.

"Wounded in Iraq or Afghanistan?"

"Iraq."

"He's a hero, too," she says. "You must be very proud of him."

"I am," Tess says.

Harold pokes at the yoke of an eggs with a fork. Pride is not what he is feeling. He stabs a piece of biscuit and rubs it in gravy before lifting it to his mouth. He swallows without an appetite. He ponders what a hero is and what makes one so. To be a hero takes more than courage and sacrifice. There must be value to a hero's cause. He wants his son to be a hero, but David is no hero. He is a victim.

Angela brings Tess steaming tea in a white cup. Tess squeezes the lemon into it and takes a sip. Harold looks at her hands cradling the cup. Her fingernails are chewed. He thinks how both of their lives are unraveling. To see her ring finger bare gives him pause.

"I'm seeing a psychiatrist," Harold says. "I'm working on some things."

"Better late than never," Tess says.

Harold lowers his gaze to the plate of eggs.

"I'm sorry, Tess," he says. "God, I'm sorry."

Tess shrugs.

"Have you seen David yet?" she says.

"No. Have you?"

"I saw him last night."

"And?"

Tess shakes her head as if trying clear it of nightmares.

"It was shocking. There's no way to prepare yourself for how he looks. He's terribly disfigured." Tears come to her eyes. "It couldn't be worse."

Harold hands her a paper napkin. She uses it to blot her cheeks. Harold pictures David without an arm and a leg, a fingerless hand, his face burned away. He remembers driving to David's fraternity house to apologize to him for the sordid episode in the motel room. David met him on the steps with a can of Coke in his hand. He had been to football practice, and he was dressed in gym shorts and a jersey with cutoff sleeves. When Harold held out his arms to hug David, he told Harold to get the hell away. As Harold pulled from the curb, David charged after Harold yelling, *I fucking hate you. I hate you.* David threw the Coke at Harold's SUV. The can exploded on the pavement like a hand grenade. One month later, David quit school. He joined the Army where he became an Airborne Ranger and volunteered to serve with the infantry in Iraq.

Harold shakes his head. The weight of his guilt bears down on his chest, restricts his ability to breathe.

"Are you sure he wants to see me?" Harold says.

"He didn't want to," Tess says. "Can't say as I blame him. But I convinced him he should." Tess drinks her tea. "He's going to need both of us to get him through this. If nothing else, we're strong. God chose us because He knows we're strong."

Harold silently scoffs at the idea of a God that ruthless. He pushes back his plate.

"Goddamn stupid war," he says. "It's like Vietnam. There's no purpose to it."

"Don't say that in front of David," Tess says. "You'll make him feel like his sacrifice was for nothing."

"It was for nothing. Nada."

"Keep it to yourself."

"Okay," Harold says. "But I'll never believe differently about this goddamn war."

He catches Angela's eye and motions for the check.

"What's David like?" he says. "What's he say about his situation? He must be terribly depressed."

"At first he tried to be stoic and make light of it. He made a horrible joke. Called himself a crispy critter. But then he broke down and cried like he was little boy again. After we both settled down and talked, the one thing that stood out was that he wants to have been a good soldier." Tess stares at her teacup as if it might contain the solution to David's plight. "We must help him to believe he was a good soldier."

Angela arrives at the table with the check and hands it to Harold. On the bill, she has drawn a happy face and written "Good Luck."

"Muchas gracias," Harold says.

He pays her in cash. Tips her well. As he pockets his wallet, Harold is thinking about David wanting to be a "good soldier." He wonders what a good soldier is and if there can be a good soldier in a bad war. It seems contradictory, even impossible, like being a good husband in a bad marriage.

HAROLD FOLLOWS Tess out of the restaurant into the inferno-like heat. A hot Texas wind blows a newspaper across a shadowless parking lot. The air is bone dry and smells of sage and burning rubber. Behind the wheel of his rented Honda, Harold drives on pavement that quivers in the heat. On the car radio, Dwight Yoakum's country twang sings, "I'm a thousand miles from nowhere. Time don't matter to me." Harold wheels into the burn center's lot and parks among olive-drab Army vehicles that bring to mind the motor pool thirty years ago when he was stationed at Fort Sam Huston here in San Antonio. He feels as if he is back in the military preparing to deploy to Vietnam.

In the corridor of the hospital, reminders of war are everywhere. A Marine in dress blues passes Harold. The young soldier's crutches strike the ground with the cadence of a funeral march. In a wheelchair, a burn patient with a ripple-scarred face pushes himself slowly, grimacing as if in pain. Harold averts his eyes. The medical staff wears fatigues with American flags on the sleeves. On the desert-beige walls, the clocks are set to the time in Iraq and Afghanistan. In silence, Harold and Tess ride an elevator to the fourth floor where the U.S. Army Institute of Surgical Research Burn Center is housed.

When they step out of the elevator, Tess says, "I never dreamed our lives would come to this."

"Me either," Harold says.

At the door of the unit, they are greeted by Alice, a sturdy blond nurse, dressed in a green scrub suit with sweat stains under her arms. Her pearl earrings dangle from long gold chains. Harold offers her his hand and introduces them as David's parents.

"Your son is getting the best care in the world," Alice says. She hands Harold and Tess paper gowns and booties to cover their shoes. She points at a canister of surgical soap above a sink. "Before you enter the unit, give your hands a good scrubbing. Infection is the burn patient's number one enemy."

"I'm a physician," Harold says. "A surgeon."

"Then you know about burns," Alice says.

"Unfortunately, I do," he says.

Harold removes the splint from his hand and begins

washing his hands. He decides to leave the splint off so as not to draw David's attention to his own lesser injury.

"David's strong," Alice said. "He's definitely a fighter. But he needs strong support from his family. We find that's the most important ingredient in our wounded warriors' recovery."

"Don't worry," Tess says. "He'll get strong support. His recovery is all that matters. It's what God wants from us now." She looks at Harold. "Isn't that right, Harold?"

"We'll do everything we can," Harold says.

The doors to the ICU spring open. Harold follows the nurse into a cacophony: the beep of monitors, the whoosh of ventilators, the rustle of the medical staff hurrying from cubical to cubical. Although he has spent years working in intensive care units, Harold feels as if he's entering a world of science fiction where he has never been before. His heart pounds against his sternum. His knees feel as if they may buckle. Be strong for David, he tells himself.

In his cubical, David lies on a hospital bed as if it were a raft with masts of IV poles. Above him, lighted waves flit across a monitor's screen. The air smells oily, a scent that Harold recognizes as Silvadene, an antibiotic burn ointment. David's bandages seem luminescent, as if they were the source of light for the room.

"In case you're wondering," David says. "It's me, David."

Harold looks at David's partially bandaged face. He has no ears and only a nubbin of a nose with gaping nostrils. His mouth is a hole surrounded by scarred lips that don't come together. On his scalp, clumps of hair protrude like weeds. Harold lowers his eyes to David's body. His right hand is missing. What remains of his left hand is wrapped in gauze. His right leg has been amputated above the knee. Somewhere Harold once read that, "It's the divine right of man to appear human." But David doesn't appear human; he appears like a reptile that has emerged from a bog. Harold wants to scream. He stifles an urge to look away and smiles at David.

"Of course, it's you, Son," Harold says.

"It's a different me," David says.

"No," Tess says. "You're our same David."

"I'm different, Mom. I only have one arm and one leg."

Tess rests her hand on David's bandaged arm. He groans.

"I'm sorry," she says, withdrawing her touch.

Harold lowers himself onto a chair. So here is my son, he thinks. In total ruin, and my recklessness is the cause of it. From a bedside stand, Harold picks up the "Hero's Handbook" and "Warrior Welcome Packet" that were issued to David yesterday on his arrival at Brooke.

Harold detests his son being known as warrior, thinks it further dehumanizes him. He drops the pamphlets back on the table in disgust.

"Do you know about what happened to me?" David says.

His voice is hoarse from the edema of his vocal cords caused by smoke inhalation, and his immobile lips form words with difficulty. Harold moves closer to him to hear.

"Some of it," he says. "Captain Keevil told me about the bomb. How they pulled you from the Humvee that was on fire."

"Everything happened so fast," David says. "After they put out the fire and before I passed out, I remember checking my body to see what was left." He shakes his head. "Man, it was weird. I thought I still had my arms and legs."

He pauses for a few second and stares at the ceiling with his nearly lidless eyes.

"Lewis was killed," he says.

"That's what Captain Keevil told me," Harold says. "It sounds like you were good buddies."

"Like brothers. Usually I drove and Lewis rode shotgun. For some reason, I insisted on him driving that night. It's not right that he's dead and I'm not."

"You shouldn't feel guilty about anything," Tess says. "You served your country well. You've made a great sacrifice for it. Lewis died with honor and you were wounded with honor. We're very proud of you."

Harold remembers his company commander in Vietnam telling the new troops in-country that death in combat is nothing but carelessness or bad luck. But looking at his son, Harold believes death would have been good luck, a blessing. Lewis was the lucky one.

Tears glisten in David's eyes.

"What's the matter, David?" Tess says.

"I'm afraid," he says.

"Don't be afraid," Tess says. "What are you afraid of?"

"Everything. The pain. All the torture I'll have to go through. What I'll be like." He looks at Harold. "What are they're going to do to me?"

"I'm going to have a meeting with your doctors," Harold says. "Then we can talk over their treatment plan." He sees the pain and fright that glaze David's eyes. "You look uncomfortable. We should let you rest. Do you need pain medicine?"

"Yeah."

At the nurses' station Harold asks Alice for a narcotic for David.

"Sure," she says. "Can I get him anything else?"

An arm and leg, Harold wants to say. His old life back.

Alice's response to the request isn't quick. When she finally appears, she apologizes about being so busy.

"That's okay," David says.

In his mouth, Alice places a plastic stick tipped with a pain killer she calls a "fentanyl pop." That David nods as a way of thanking her makes Harold proud.

"You're a true warrior," Alice says. "We're going to get you through this."

David nods. He sucks the morphine-like drug while Alice palpates the radial pulse in his only wrist. Harold remembers David as boy with an orange popsicle. At four, David was an Indian chief, at five a fireman. When he was six, he was a magician who could make himself disappear by drinking a glass of juice. Harold wishes David had that power now. He would find him a glass of juice. David grunts. Alice takes the stick from him and drops it in a glass on the table.

"Feel better?" she says.

"Got a buzz going."

Harold sees that the fentanyl has constricted David's pupils to pinpoint size and slurred his speech.

"Good for you," Harold says. "Now rest. We'll see you later."

In a few seconds, David's eyes roll up under what remains of their lids. His breathing deepens and slows. Thank God for opiates, Harold thinks, the kindest medicine there is.

Tess bends over David.

"My baby," she whispers.

Suddenly Harold's eyes glisten. At the door, he turns back and looks at David asleep. If only I had . . . Without completing the thought, Harold wishes David's pain were his.

IN THE LATE AFTERNOON, Harold has the burn center's waiting room all to himself. He sits on a hard plastic chair under the ubiquitous photograph of President George W. Bush. A television mounted on the wall is turned so he can't see it. The dirty, mullioned windows remind him of a jail. He has been there for nearly an hour, waiting to meet with Lt. Colonel Cassidy, the surgeon in charge of David's care. Harold tries to read a magazine article about vintage guitars. Unable to concentrate, he puts it aside. He slides down in the chair and closes his eyes. Suddenly, he hears the hydraulic swish of the unit's doors springing open. Harold rises in nervous anticipation. Alice, David's nurse, appears. With one hand on an arm and another around a waist, she supports a red-haired woman in a cheap cotton maternity dress. The expectant mother looks no older than a high school girl. She sobs uncontrollably, her chest and big belly heaving. Alice wraps her arms around the grief-stricken woman and hugs her. Harold watches Alice's eyes fill with tears. He admires her tender air and contrasts it with his own avoidance of intimacy with patients.

When the new widow walks past Harold, he casts his eyes toward the floor.

Goddamn Iraq, he thinks. Goddamn Afghanistan. Goddamn Vietnam. Goddamn war.

When he looks up, Alice is coming toward him. Sorrow and exhaustion crease her soft round face. The shoulder of her scrub shirt is wet with tears. Harold rises to greet her.

"Sorry you're having to wait so long," she says. "We've been dealing with an emergency. Colonel Cassidy will be here soon."

"A death?" Harold says.

"Yeah. Nineteen years old."

"How do you do it day after day?" Harold says.

"On my way home, there's a spot where I pull off the road. I sit there awhile and gather myself before I go in the house and see my kids. I don't want to take things home."

Harold nods.

"You've been through this a lot," Alice says. "How do you handle it when you lose a patient?"

"I kick a wastebasket," he says.

Suddenly, grief buffets him like an unsuspected wave

in the surf. He eyes glisten with tears. Alice rests her hand on his shoulder.

"Are you okay?" she says.

"Not totally," he says. "I'm kind of worn thin."

Alice returns to the unit, and soon Colonel Cassidy appears. For a moment, he takes a measure of the room. Then he comes to Harold very quickly. Harold holds out his left hand, and they shake. The doctor is short but imposing with a gray burr cut. His body is taut, his back straight. He has something of a Weimaraner's face with sunken cheeks and pale penetrating eyes. He sits on the edge of a chair as if he is about to jump up and run.

"Thank you for your time," Harold says.

"What can I tell you?" Cassidy says.

"My son David wants to know what's in store for him," Harold says. "I'd like for you to go over your treatment plan so I can help him understand."

Cassidy nods. He fingers the pager clipped to the waist of his scrub suit.

"Well," he says, "to say the least, David's injuries are extensive. It's miraculous he's alive. His reconstruction could be a residency for a plastic surgeon."

Harold nods. He considers Cassidy's manner courteous but cold.

"The first order of business is to get skin coverage of his burns. It will require multiple split thickness grafts.

That's where a thin piece of good skin is shaved from the patient and transplanted to a burned area."

"I know about skin grafts," Harold says. "I'm a general surgeon. I served in Vietnam as a battalion surgeon with the 9th Infantry."

"Well, then," Cassidy says, "you understand wounds."

"The pathophysiology of them but not the *why* of them. Have you been in combat?"

"Iraq and Afghanistan twice."

"So you know what it was like where David was," Harold says.

"All too well." Cassidy's pager hums. He silences it with the press of a button. "In your son's case, there aren't many unburned donor sites available. But we'll find skin somewhere. We could even use the soles of his feet."

"Foot," Harold says.

"Right. Sorry," Cassidy says. "After he gets healed up, we can start reconstruction of his face. His eyelids come first. His ears and lips are going to need work, but that's down the road. He has an unburned island of skin on his forehead where his helmet must have protected him. It could make a nice flap to build a nose with."

"You know," Harold says. "He used to look like me, only better."

For a moment, Cassidy's expression softens, and he looks thoughtfully at Harold.

"This must be hard for you," the colonel says. "Knowing what you know surely makes it worse."

"It's hard beyond description. What about his extremities? The contractures of his neck and arm. He needs to know it all."

"You're right about the contractures," Cassidy says. "The one of the left elbow will need to be released with a Z-plasty, and his neck scars as well. The amputation of his leg needs a revision so a prosthesis will fit properly."

Harold listens. He tries to block out that it is his son whom Cassidy is condemning to a life of hell.

"He'll need plenty of physical therapy for strength and gait training. The prosthetics they have now are miraculous. Your son will master them in no time. Before you know it, he'll be playing ball."

"The hand," Harold says. "What about a hand? Of everything that is missing, it's a hand he needs most."

"When I revise the amputated fingers on his remaining hand, I'll try to leave a nubbin, so he can button his shirt and go to the bathroom. To replace his missing arm, he'll be fitted with a myoelectric prosthesis, a new human-like arm we're using now."

Human-like, Harold thinks. How dehumanizing.

"Arm transplantation is being tried at some centers in Europe," Cassidy says. "It's in its infancy. Right now, rejection is particularly problematic. But David may eventually be a candidate for transplantation if the right donor can be found. In the years ahead, many new things will be available to make him whole."

Harold sits staring at his own hand. He wiggles his fingers and watches them move. He's made a small fortune with those hands.

"So how many operations are we looking at?" Harold says.

"Fifteen. Twenty. It could be more. I don't like to make predictions."

"My Lord," Harold says. "This will take years. A lifetime."

"The way I approach these soldiers is a day at a time," Cassidy says. "The big picture is overwhelming. We look for small successes that will help them be functional. These guys are incredibly stoic. What they want is to be able to take care of themselves. Little successes can make all the difference in the world."

"You know," Harold says. "There's a hell of lot more that David wanted out of life than to be functional. He had nearly perfect SATs. He was a hell of football player. He was a premed. He was a big-hearted kid who did for people. He looked forward to things. He had big dreams for himself like you must have had."

"Unfortunately," Cassidy says, "sometimes we have to reel in our dreams."

Harold shakes his head. He starts to ask Cassidy if he has children, then changes his mind. Harold sits for a moment, thinking of the complications David is likely to encounter: infection, renal failure, bedsores, phantom pains, post traumatic stress syndrome, depression, addiction. He remembers Tess saying that God chose David to be injured because we are strong and will pass His test. He wonders why, if God only selects the strong to suffer, have so many veterans cracked under the weight of their wounds. It 's more likely that David's suffering is some kind of holy vengeance.

"Tell me something, Cassidy," Harold says. "Why the fuck do you think this happened to my son?"

"I'll tell you why, Sir. Because there are Jihadists who want to end our way of life. Surely, you remember 911. There are evil forces in this world. Your son opposed them. That's why he got hurt."

"Nothing in the world justifies the trauma inflicted on David," Harold says.

"All I can say," Cassidy says, "is that your son is a great American."

Harold hates Cassidy. The Army. The war. His son's wounds. Himself. He looks up at the major.

"One more question. Then I'll let you go," Harold says. "Do you really think it is right to put David through all this hell?"

"I never give up on anybody," Cassidy says.

〜

LATER IN THE DAY, Harold invites Tess to join him for dinner on the Riverwalk. Before he talks with David, he wants to discuss with her what he learned from Cassidy. He thinks that if they could spend some time together, she might have a change of heart and want him back. But Tess declines. She tells him she has already made plans to eat with women she met at the gazebo, a gathering place on the hospital's grounds where mothers and wives of wounded soldiers come to commiserate.

When Harold leaves the hospital, he sees Tess under the hexagonal roof with her new friends. To see her puffing on a cigarette startles Harold. She hasn't smoked in thirty years. He thinks of her and the other women as collateral damage—like the mothers of My Lai.

Harold eats at the Lone Star Cafe, a Texas grill where the hostess says "Howdy" and kids eat for free on Thursdays. His table on the patio overlooks the San Antonio River. Its water is brown with foamy flotsam. Harold sips a salty margarita and watches families with young children drift by on barges. The memory of what his own little family once was haunts him. He recalls things about Tess he admires: her ability to take life in stride and be in touch with her feelings, her optimism, her artistic eye that sees things in a different way than he does. She seems to somehow have a grasp on the essence of life that he doesn't possess. He wonders if he could change, control his appetites, and find God? Would she forgive him?

Harold orders chicken-fried chicken, but the waitress serves him chicken-fried steak. The sour slaw and Ménage À Trois merlot give him heartburn. With the splint on his hand, he has difficulty cutting his meat. At a nearby table, a bearded bald man in white cowboy boots dines with a young voluptuous Hispanic woman in a denim miniskirt and harsh makeup. Harold thinks she must be from one of the escort services—like "Sweet Sensations" or "Secret Pleasures"—he's Googled on the internet. Somewhere down the street, a Mariachi band plays "La Diferencia." Harold had hoped for music, preferably acoustic guitar, but the blare of the trumpet only adds to his loneliness.

After dinner, Harold drives to a shopping center on the edge of town. A bank thermometer registers 104 degrees. His hand is swollen and aches. At Alamo City Liquors, he buys a six pack of Dos Equis. With an open can of beer between his legs, he heads northwest on Military Highway, a smooth straight road, through scrub pines and sandy hills.

When Harold was stationed at Fort Sam, he received a cursory basic training to prepare him to be a medical officer in a combat zone. Fresh out of internship, he learned the rudiments of military protocol: whom and how to salute, the difference between a "Light" and "Bird" Colonel, the importance of polished shoes and belt buckles. Dressed in new summer khakis and a garrison cap, he marched in the morning and listened to lectures on tropical medicine and triage. In the afternoon, he operated on goats shot with high powered rifles so he could learn to handle the peculiarities of high velocity wounds. The last week of his training was spent in the field at Camp Bullis, a wasteland of desert and low hills near San Antonio. A tall Black drill sergeant ordered Harold to belly crawl under machine gun fire and to take target practice with an M16 and a semiautomatic .45 caliber revolver. At night, Harold, in camouflage fatigues and jungle boots, stumbled around in the dark with a compass, lost on the night map reading and land navigation exercise.

Now, Harold pulls his dust-coated Honda onto a narrow side road that overlooks Camp Bullis's desolate acreage. He climbs out of the car onto gravel that is like a bed of coals. The heat buzzes and presses down on him. Harold sits on the car's hood. He rolls a can of beer across his forehead. He pops the tab and drinks. He remembers another hot Texas night in '67 during a weekend break in basic training. With three other newly commissioned medical officers, he drove his Buick convertible with the top down from Fort Sam to "Boy's Town" in Nuevo Laredo, Mexico. The young doctors were all about to go to war, and nothing seemed to matter. In the La Zona Rosa, they got drunk on shots of tequila and whored at the Casino El Papagayo, a seedy bar with connected rooms. Harold tries to recall what the girl was like, the position of their bodies, the scent of her. Like so many of his liaisons, she has departed his memory. But Katya remains like a malignant neoplasm in the cortex of his brain. Once he read something by Mailer that said, "Guilt is the existential edge of sex. Without guilt, sex is meaningless." Harold wonders if he acts out in defiance of his guilt.

Before him, the desert sinks, vast and parched, devoid of man or God. In the distance, black hillocks stand dimensionless against a mauve sky. Overhead turkey vultures circle on thermals. Heat lightening flares like white phosphorus rounds. It reminds him of the flash and boom of war. Harold thinks creatures can only survive by preying on one another.

For a while he ponders what Colonel Cassidy told him David will have to endure, the painful operations, the brutal rehabilitation. David's war isn't over; it's only beginning. Harold recalls how David's intelligence, his looks, and athleticism once defined him. In the future, his wounds will define him, just as Harold's own self-inflicted wounds now define him.

Harold stares at his hands and tries to imagine what it would be like without them. He brings his thumb over to his index finger. It is the ability to grip and grasp and torque that sets humans apart from lower forms of life. He forces himself to think of what David still has rather than what he is missing. But his thoughts always return to David's wounds. It seems senseless for David to go on living.

Harold drinks and stares out at the darkening desert, a landscape too large for him to understand. The air squeezes hot on him. His sweat-soaked madras shirt clings to his barrel chest. The mauve sky bleeds into the horizon and turns pale ghostly gray. Harold feels like a forward observer at dusk. Among merging shadows of the sagebrush, Harold thinks he sees a Humvee moving slowly through shimmering heat. A burst of light consumes the vehicle. Harold lowers his head into his hands. When he looks up at the desert again, the Humvee has vanished.

IN THE MORNING, Harold skips breakfast to arrive at David's cubicle before Tess. He has come early to spend time alone with his son. The fluorescent light makes David's bandages appear blue. At the bedside, two heat lamps have been aimed to warm him because his burns have disrupted his body's thermostat, and he can't maintain his core temperature. The room is like a pottery kiln, even hotter than it is outside. Harold wants to hug David, but he knows the slightest movement or touch gives David pain. So he grasps the toes of David's only foot and gives them a squeeze. David returns the gesture with a wiggle of his foot.

Harold settles into a straight-back chair beside the bed. For a moment, he studies David with a clinical eye. He sees that the catheter bag collecting his urine is nearly overflowing. He assumes David is in the diuretic phase of the burn injury and is mobilizing body fluids. His heart monitor shows a rapid heart rate, the tachycardia of stress and plasma depletion. Harold is struck by how thin David is, his muscle mass already wasting away. What remains of his once powerful body is like a cut of meat, no more to it than a side of ribs.

"Met with your doctor last evening," Harold says. "He outlined your treatment plan. I want to go over it with you when your mother arrives. She wants to hear it, too. There are choices to be made."

"By whom?"

"You, of course."

In spite of the heat, a shiver passes through David's body.

"How was your night, son?" Harold says. "You able to sleep?"

"Nights are tough," David says in his scratchy voice. "Full of flashbacks and nightmares. Last night, I dreamed of Lewis. We were in our hooch drinking Red Bull, and he asked me what I wanted on my tombstone."

"What was your answer?"

"David Roberts: He was a good soldier."

Harold nods.

"What do you want on your tombstone?" David says.

For a moment, Harold fans himself with a folded magazine.

"Harold Roberts: He was a good father."

"Good fathers don't whore around."

Harold regrets his answer. He wishes he could disappear from the world.

"I know that," he says.

"What you did was so fucking selfish," David says. "It ruined everything. Why did you do it?"

"All I know is that I caved in to temptation. Maybe I believed because I was a doctor I was a force for good and could do anything I wanted to. Whatever made me do it, I'm deeply sorry. Now I'm trying to understand myself and change. I know there is nothing I can say to make it right to you. I just hope there is something I can do to earn your forgiveness."

A long uncomfortable silence follows. The heat in the room makes it hard for Harold to breathe. He wets a washcloth with ice water from a pitcher on a bedside table with wheels. He mops his own face with the cool cloth.

Finally, he says, "What was it like in Iraq? If you feel like talking about it."

"I despised everything there was about the place. The heat. The dust. The stink. I hate to admit it, I didn't even like the people. They wanted to kill me, and I wanted to kill them. They weren't human to me. They were ragheads. And I wasn't a human to them."

"That's war," Harold says. "If it wasn't, a decent man couldn't be a soldier."

"When I joined up," David says. "I wanted to help make the world better. But after I was there awhile, the only thing that mattered was the guys in my unit. We were a brotherhood. Iraq. America. Sunni, Shiite. Weapons of mass destruction. All of that didn't mean shit. We weren't fighting for ideas. We were fighting for the love of each other. Our reason for existence was to protect one another. That's why Lewis's death hit me so hard. I feel like I failed him." David glances at a glass on the bedside stand. "It was so dry there. Just thinking about that goddamn place makes me thirsty. Could you get me a drink, Dad?"

Harold fills the glass with ice water. He bends over David and inserts a straw into his mouth. He holds the glass for him. Unable to seal his scorched lips, David drinks with difficulty and water trickles out his mouth onto his chin. Harold smells a fruity pear-like odor rising from the bandages. He recognizes the scent of

pseudomonas, a dangerous bacterium that often infects third-degree burns. Sepsis, he thinks. Harold knows David's immune system has been depleted by the massive insult to his body. He checks the label on David's plastic IV bag and sees that he is receiving a high dose of potassium and Tobramycin, a powerful antibiotic. Reminded of his son's tenuous state, Harold shakes his head.

David pushes the straw from his mouth with his tongue. He tries to turn onto his side. He grimaces and moans. Harold thinks if he could give David a big slug of morphine in the IV, the suffering would end.

When he finds a more comfortable position, David says, "You never talk about Vietnam, Dad. What was it like for you in Nam?"

Harold senses a hint of forgiveness in the way David is calling him "Dad." For a moment, images of Vietnam come to him: Sappers with satchel charges running pell-mell through his base camp while he wonders *Am I going to live through this?* A medevac chopper hovering above him as he waits in a cloud of dust for wounded GIs. A Cambodian boom-boom girl he bought Saigon teas and danced with in a bar in Bien Hoa. Operating through the night in a sandbagged bunker. The memories seem to be of dreams.

"I felt the same about my war as you felt about yours. Why it was being fought didn't matter a damn to me either. All that mattered was helping guys like you who got messed up. The difference between you and me was our MOS. I was a noncombatant. I didn't have to go out on patrol. I didn't have to kill anyone. As far as the Vietnamese people went, I actually liked them. I guess because I was a doctor, the Army didn't bother to demonize them. What you did took a hell of lot more courage than what I did."

"I wasn't brave," David says. "I was just numb. Sort of like detached. Every time we went out, you didn't know when you were going to get hit. I was scared to death. It was just something I had to do, and I did it."

"Without fear," Harold says, "there can't be courage. Believe me, son. You were brave."

David grows quiet again. Harold looks at David's sad, lidless eyes, sees the sorrow and pain in them.

"Do you need a fentanyl pop?" he asks.

"Naw, I'm okay for now. I want to have my wits about me when I hear what I have to go through." David turns toward Harold. "Tell me something, Dad. Do you think I'll be able to work?" He hesitates for a moment. "Do you think a woman other than Mom would ever love me?"

The questions hang heavily in the sweltering, medicinal air. Harold glances at David. The depressions in the sheet where the humps of an arm and leg should be. His destroyed face. His wounds wound Harold's soul. He wishes there was something he could give David. A good arm. A new face. The love of a woman.

Harold starts to say things have a way of working out. But he reconsiders and says, "To be honest, I don't know."

"Thanks for being honest for a change."

"From now on, I'll always be honest with you."

TESS ENTERS THE CUBICAL CAUTIOUSLY. She wears a pale green hospital gown and paper hat that seem like a costume to Harold. Her presence somehow disarms him. He rises quickly from his chair. She gives him an ironic half-smile, part warmth, part distance. He feels a tug of desire that he doesn't understand. He wants to touch her but doesn't. Tess turns to David and places her hand on his foot.

"How was your night?" she says.

"Slept like a baby," David says.

Except for flashbacks and nightmares, Harold thinks. He offers Tess his chair. He stands awkwardly at the bedside. He feels so hot. A rash of sweat beads on Harold's forehead. He doesn't know how David tolerates the heat or anything else.

"Let's go, Dad," David says. "You're on. The floor is yours."

There is a tightness in Harold's stomach. He clears his throat and begins the litany of surgeries that await David. As if seeking informed consent from one of his own patients, he takes his time explaining the details of each procedure, the risks and rewards, the possible complications. He draws diagrams of a Z-plasty and a trapezoid skin flap on an envelope to illustrate how David's scar contractures will be released. Just the telling of all David will have to endure demoralizes Harold. With his eyes on the ceiling, David listens silently, impassively. On the monitor screen above his head, the signal of his heartbeat marches along.

When Harold talks about the prosthesis to replace David's missing hand, David lifts his own fingerless hand from the bed and studies it.

"I can live with a bad face," David says. "But I can't imagine going through life without a functioning hand."

"I don't have experience with these new hand prostheses to know what they can do," Harold says. "But I do know they are performing hand transplantation now with some success. Maybe you'll be a candidate for that someday."

Last night when Harold returned from the desert, he watched an animation of a hand transplant procedure on YouTube. The plating together of the radial and ulnar bones. The suturing of flexor and extensor tendons. The anastomosis of arteries, veins, and nerves with sutures as fine as cobwebs. For a moment, an idea that both excited and frightened Harold came to him. He looked down at his own hand with its rivulets of blue veins and glove of old, wrinkled skin. He flexed his fingers and watched the tendons tug and slide. He thought of all the skills embodied in his hand. What a marvelous machine it was. He wondered if those skills were somehow stored in its nerves and muscles and could be passed on.

"The key is a good genetic match with the donor," Harold says. "You must have compatible tissue types, or the graft will be rejected."

"I'm not going to get my hopes up too high," David says.

"Wouldn't that be wonderful," Tess says. "A new hand. What a gift."

With a faint smile, Harold nods. "This is going to be a long ordeal," he says. "Many operations. There will be pain and setbacks. It will be very hard. How do you feel about it?"

David is quiet for what seems like a long time. Then he lifts his head from the pillow and turns his face toward Harold. His burns not covered by gauze are weeping and blistered.

"You know," he says. "When I was playing football and the game was close and all, I would say in the huddle, 'Give me the ball. No one can take me down.'

That's the way I feel now. I want the ball. I want to live. If that's what you're asking."

Harold feels David's will and strength like wind pushing him from behind. Goose bumps rise on the back of his neck.

David lets his head drop back onto the pillow. He stares at the ceiling.

"I want to live," he says. "But only if I'm not a burden. I just want to be able to take care of myself. That's all I'm asking."

"Oh, David," Tess says. "You won't be a burden." She strokes David's foot. "No matter what, you'll never be a burden."

"We're in this together," Harold says. "We're with you all the way."

"You say *we*," David says. "Does that mean you and Mom are back together?"

Harold glances at Tess, and she looks away.

"As far as you're concerned, David," she says. "We're together."

Harold thinks of forgiveness in a family. How it is earned and what it would take to make it last.

"You're a good soldier, son," he says. "God, you're a good soldier."

# ACKNOWLEDGMENTS

I offer special thanks to Sena Jeter Naslund, a master teacher and writer, who has been my mentor and close friend for many years. Without her guidance and encouragement, this book would not have been possible.

I wish also to thank my writer friends, Lucinda Sullivan, Bill Pearce, and Barb Shoup, who read these stories and gave me invaluable editorial advice. I give thanks to Lou Ann Walker, my cousin, dear friend, and editor, to my agent, Sterling Lord, and to Karen Mann, who was the original editor of this collection when it was first published by Fleur-de-Lis Press.

I wish to thank my daughters—Beth, Sarah, and Katie—and my sister Sandra for their love and support, and most especially my mother Betty, who taught me to read and love the written word.

And, finally, I wish to express my gratitude to Toni Wolcott, for her love, her constant encouragement, and fine editorial eye. This book is dedicated to her.

# ABOUT THE AUTHOR

Daly Walker grew up in Winchester, Indiana. He received a B.A. from Ohio Wesleyan University and an M.D. from Indiana University. He served his surgery residency at the University of Wisconsin. He is a fellow in the American College of Surgery. For thirty-five years, he practiced general surgery in Columbus, Indiana. He has three daughters: Beth, Sarah, and Katie. He was a battalion surgeon with the Army in Vietnam where he received a Bronze Star. He studied creative writing at Indiana University and the University of Louisville. His stories and essays have appeared in numerous literary publications, including *The Atlantic Monthly, The Sewanee Review, The Louisville Review, The Sycamore Review,* and *The Southampton Review*. His fiction has been anthologized in *Faith Stories,* edited by Michael Curtis, *Story Matters,* and the *Bedford Introduction to Literature*. For many years, he has been represented by the literary agent Sterling Lord. Daly's work has been shortlisted for *Best American Short Stories* and an O'Henry Award, and one of his stories was a finalist in stories chosen for *The Best American Magazine Writing* anthology. Now retired from medicine, he divides his time between Quechee, Vermont and Boca Grande, Florida.